"The name LEANNE BANKS signifies
the very best in romance."
—*Romantic Times Magazine*

**SILHOUETTE DESIRE IS PROUD TO
PRESENT A BRAND-NEW MINISERIES BY
BESTSELLING AUTHOR LEANNE BANKS**

The legendary Logans
face their greatest challenge,
each seeking a love that lasts forever....

**Her Forever Man (SD #1267)
—on sale January 2000
The Doctor Wore Spurs (SD #1280)
—on sale March 2000
Expecting His Child (SD #1292)
—on sale May 2000**

Don't miss any of these Silhouette Desire novels!

Dear Reader,

Please join us in celebrating Silhouette's 20th anniversary in 2000! We promise to deliver—all year—passionate, powerful, provocative love stories from your favorite Desire authors!

This January, look for bestselling author Leanne Banks's first MAN OF THE MONTH with *Her Forever Man.* Watch sparks fly when irresistibly rugged ranch owner Brock Logan comes face-to-face with his new partner, the fiery Felicity Chambeau, in the first book of Leanne's brand-new miniseries LONE STAR FAMILIES: THE LOGANS.

Desire is pleased to continue the Silhouette cross-line continuity ROYALLY WED with *The Pregnant Princess* by favorite author Anne Marie Winston. After a night of torrid passion with a stranger, a beautiful princess ends up pregnant…and seeks out the father of her child.

Elizabeth Bevarly returns to Desire with her immensely popular miniseries FROM HERE TO MATERNITY with *Dr. Mommy,* about a couple reunited by a baby left on a doorstep. *Hard Lovin' Man,* another of Peggy Moreland's TEXAS BRIDES, captures the intensity of falling in love when a cowgirl gives her heart to a sweet-talkin', hard-lovin' hunk. Cathleen Galitz delivers a compelling marriage-of-convenience tale in *The Cowboy Takes a Bride,* in the series THE BRIDAL BID. And Sheri WhiteFeather offers another provocative Native American hero in *Skyler Hawk: Lone Brave.*

Help us celebrate 20 years of great romantic fiction from Silhouette by indulging yourself with all six delectably sensual Desire titles each and every month during this special year!

Enjoy!

Joan Marlow Golan
Senior Editor, Silhouette Desire

Please address questions and book requests to:
Silhouette Reader Service
U.S.: 3010 Walden Ave., P.O. Box 1325, Buffalo, NY 14269
Canadian: P.O. Box 609, Fort Erie, Ont. L2A 5X3

Her Forever Man

LEANNE BANKS

Published by Silhouette Books

America's Publisher of Contemporary Romance

If you purchased this book without a cover you should be aware that this book is stolen property. It was reported as "unsold and destroyed" to the publisher, and neither the author nor the publisher has received any payment for this "stripped book."

Special acknowledgment and thanks to Susan Macias for lighting a candle for me when things got a little dark and to the TCU School of Ranch Management for educating me about the cattle business.

This book is dedicated to two groups of fabulous ladies I'm blessed to know: The Relay for Life Pink Ribbon Runners and the Desire Loop.

 SILHOUETTE BOOKS

ISBN 0-373-76267-4

HER FOREVER MAN

Copyright © 2000 by Leanne Banks

All rights reserved. Except for use in any review, the reproduction or utilization of this work in whole or in part in any form by any electronic, mechanical or other means, now known or hereafter invented, including xerography, photocopying and recording, or in any information storage or retrieval system, is forbidden without the written permission of the editorial office, Silhouette Books, 300 East 42nd Street, New York, NY 10017 U.S.A.

All characters in this book have no existence outside the imagination of the author and have no relation whatsoever to anyone bearing the same name or names. They are not even distantly inspired by any individual known or unknown to the author, and all incidents are pure invention.

This edition published by arrangement with Harlequin Books S.A.

® and TM are trademarks of Harlequin Books S.A., used under license. Trademarks indicated with ® are registered in the United States Patent and Trademark Office, the Canadian Trade Marks Office and in other countries.

Visit us at www.romance.net

Printed in U.S.A.

LEANNE BANKS

is a national number-one bestselling author of romance. She lives in her native Virginia with her husband, son and daughter. Recognized for both her sensual and humorous writing with two Career Achievement Awards from *Romantic Times Magazine,* Leanne likes creating a story with a few grins, a generous kick of sensuality and characters that hang around after the book is finished. Leanne believes romance readers are the best readers in the world because they understand that love is the greatest miracle of all. You can write to her at P.O. Box 1442, Midlothian, VA 23113. A SASE for a reply would be greatly appreciated.

Four generations ago, the Logan family moved west from Virginia and took a scrap of Texas land. Despite droughts and floods, broken hearts and death, the Logans now own one of the most successful cattle ranches in Texas.

The Logans have power, brains and strength. Some call their ongoing success a legacy. The Logans would instead point to hard work, persistence and plain old American ingenuity. When it comes to matters of the heart, however, they refer to their inheritance as a curse. The Logans face their greatest challenge in breaking that curse, and finding a love that lasts forever....

Prologue

All Brock Logan wanted was a smooth-running ranch, security for his children, and peace.

He wasn't interested in excitement or the foolishness of romance. He'd experienced the curse of passion firsthand when his ex-wife left him with a broken heart and two kids to raise. He thought of his kids and inhaled a breath of air tinged with the metallic scent of impending rain. Thank God for his son and daughter.

All he really wanted was peace. Standing on the wooden porch of the sprawling home his forefathers had built and he had expanded, he eyed the dark, angry-looking clouds coming in from the north. He crumpled the fax in his fist as uneasiness curled in his gut.

"We could use the rain," his younger brother Tyler

said, joining Brock on the porch. "But I couldn't tell it from your face."

"We don't need a quick storm. We need a long, soaking rain. We don't need a flighty visitor, either," he muttered, glancing at the fax in his hand.

"Visitor," Tyler echoed. "Who's that fax from?"

Brock's stomach tightened again. "Greg Roberts, our attorney." *Wuss* attorney, he thought. Brock knew Greg had faxed instead of called to avoid Brock's wrath. Brock had wanted to dissolve the silly silent partner agreement years ago, but Greg had dragged his feet. "He says our silent partner's paying us a visit."

Tyler blinked. "Silent partner? Not the Chambeaus?"

"Chambeau," Brock corrected and narrowed his eyes. "There's only one Chambeau left. Felicity Chambeau." He unfolded the fax and reread it. "Her attorney contacted Greg and told him she would like to visit the dwelling set aside as part of the contractual agreement between her great-great-grandfather and our great-great-grandfather."

Tyler frowned in confusion. "Isn't that *dwelling* where the foreman is living?"

Brock nodded and pulled his hat off his head. He raked his fingers through his hair. "Yep, and since he's a product of TCU Ranch Management School, I want to keep him happy. This could be a rough calving season since the Coltrane bull sowed his oats in one of my pastures. Looks like it's gonna be rough in more than one way."

"Where's she going to stay?"

Brock kissed his peace good-bye. "In the house.

There's no decent hotels in Blackstone,'' he said, referring to the closest town.

Tyler chuckled. "Maybe she'll liven things up around here.''

Brock glowered at his brother. "I don't need to have things livened up.''

All Felicity Chambeau wanted was to give away half of her money, she thought as she wearily stared out the window of her cab at the unfamiliar terrain. She knew her money was useless sitting in the bank gaining interest, and she had reached the conclusion that it was her purpose in life to give it away to a worthy cause. Besides, she wanted off that blasted list. The one that, without fail, annually listed the fifty wealthiest women in America. As long as she was on the stupid list, she might as well be wearing a bull's-eye for every opportunistic male acquainted with the knowledge of her wealth.

Although she hadn't excelled at anything else in life, surely this couldn't be that difficult. Somehow, however, she'd bungled this, too.

Her attorneys had recommended she go somewhere quiet until some of the scandal died down and they made progress with the legal proceedings. When Felicity thought of quiet, she pictured a nice little château in the south of France. Her attorneys preferred something in the south, but more domestic should she need to testify. Texas.

It might as well have been a foreign country to her. Accustomed to a Manhattan skyline, she found the endless flat plain and swollen gray skies desolate and too quiet. Even the cab driver was quiet. The quiet made her want to run.

Closing her eyes, she took a deep breath and leaned back in her seat. Maybe all her running had gotten her into trouble. After her parents had died, she'd run from one charity event to the next. Stay busy, avoid the pain, don't look in the mirror, dodge the loss, shake the emptiness and the rootless feeling in her life. Running was easier. She'd run into the open arms of her financial advisor Douglas. She'd trusted Douglas, believed him, and he had left the country with a tidy portion of her money and an exotic dancer named Chi Chi. All of this caused quite a scandal, and although she was far from broke, she felt very close to broken.

She swallowed the bitter taste of shame on her tongue. She was more disappointed in herself than in Doug. All her running had led her nowhere. Opening her eyes, she glanced at the endless flat plain. Now, she was in Nowhere, Texas.

Maybe it was time to stop running.

Maybe it was time to face Felicity.

The prospect filled her with apprehension. Most of her life she'd felt alone. Doug wasn't the only man who'd taught her that no man would ever love her for herself, so she might as well give up the idea of getting married. That was fine, but she still wanted off that infernal list. After that, what would be left?

Felicity would be stuck with Felicity.

Her stomach twisted in fear. What if she didn't like what she saw in the mirror? What if she didn't like what she learned about herself? What if she came up lacking? Felicity took a careful, determined breath and narrowed her eyes. If she didn't like what she learned, then perhaps somehow, she'd find a way to change.

The monotony of the setting might be good, she mused. There would obviously be no distractions.

One

He was *big*.

With the rain falling in sheets and her cab driver honking his horn, Felicity stood on the Logans' front porch and met the unwelcome laser-blue gaze of a tall, muscular man. It was more than height; everything about him looked overwhelmingly strong—starting with his jaw. His shoulders were broad, his large hands rested on narrow denim-clad hips that emphasized his powerful thighs and long legs. He looked like a no-nonsense, hard-nosed man who wouldn't put up with any foolishness, let alone a down-on-her-luck woman from New York.

Thunder cracked through the air, and Felicity flinched. She'd never liked thunderstorms. She took a careful breath and tried to smile. "Hello, I'm Felicity Chambeau." She didn't offer her hand. He might crush it. Ridiculous thought, but it was dark, she was tired, and he was just so big.

"You're early," he said, his gaze falling over her.

In her damp state, Felicity felt certain she came up short in his assessment. "I—I—" She clamped her mouth shut. She might have her share of shortcomings, but stuttering because a big man was giving her a hard glance wasn't one of them. "My attorneys contacted your attorney several times during the last few weeks. It's such a dreary evening. I don't want to impose. If you could just direct me to my quarters…"

"My foreman, his wife, their two kids and one-week-old baby are in your quarters."

Felicity blinked. "Oh."

"I could ask them to move somewhere else," he said.

"Oh, no," Felicity said, at a loss. "You can't do that."

He nodded. "You'll stay here."

With him? Felicity swallowed. He appeared as pleased about the prospect as she felt. "And you are Mr. Logan?"

"Brock Logan," he said, turning his head slightly.

She saw the scar on his cheek, a bold jagged stroke about an inch long that might upset an artist, but made Felicity curious. He whistled at the cab driver and firmly pointed toward the porch. Her driver swiftly unloaded her three suitcases, hanging bag and carry-on bag.

Felicity paid the driver and glanced up to catch Brock Logan staring at her luggage in dismay, then rubbing his hand over his forehead.

He took a step forward, and she instinctively

stepped backward. He took another step forward which she matched in the opposite direction. He narrowed his eyes, and she took one more step. But there was no ground beneath her foot.

"Oh, no!" She fell, silently cursing the clumsiness that had dogged her every year she'd been on this earth, but strong hands stopped her from hitting her knees. Her face mere inches from the apex of his thighs, she swallowed at the nearness of his masculinity encased in worn denim. He smelled of clean musk and leather. He was unabashedly male, and Felicity was accustomed to men who cloaked their gender in gentler, more ambiguous, contemporary ways. She closed her eyes to get her bearings. Heaven help her, this was not a good start.

His hands lifted her, pulling her up, almost skimming the length of his frame. Felicity's heart pounded with apprehension and something else she couldn't name. His hands were firm yet gentle. There would be no bruises from his touch.

For one sliver of a second, she felt the rare impact of controlled strength in his fingers and glimpsed something even more rare in his eyes. Honor. Felicity hadn't thought that quality existed anymore. Her stomach took another dip.

"Thank you," she managed in a whisper.

He shrugged and released her, then, grabbing the three suitcases, he swept through the door. "This way," he said.

She forced her feet to move, climbing a curved wooden staircase with a brass banister. She moved quickly, catching blurred impressions of the house; space, soft light, polished wood, warmth. Photographs and portraits lined the walls of the stairway, and Felicity immediately absorbed the strong sense of family tradition.

"Breakfast at 6:00 a.m.," Brock said, "dinner at 6:00 p.m., lunch on your own. If you make a meal in the kitchen, clean up after yourself. My housekeeper's touchy about messes she doesn't make."

In other words, don't expect chocolates on the pillow, she thought, following him into a small bedroom with an antique double bed, dresser, bureau and nightstand. He flicked on the bedside lamp. "The bathroom's down the hall."

"Your home is lovely." She stroked the cherry wood of the dresser. "The furniture isn't western."

"My ancestors were from Virginia."

Felicity nodded. "Your wife or decorator did a marvelous job with—"

"I don't have a wife," he said bluntly, his eyes turning hard. "I do have two kids, though. Bree and Jacob aren't known for being quiet, but I'll tell them to stay out of your way. My brother Tyler is a doctor, but he's here as often as he is in town. My sister Martina is in Chicago working for a computer company, but she can stop in at any moment. Our housekeeper's name is Addie. She keeps things running smoothly, so I'd appreciate it if you didn't upset her."

Felicity digested the information and nodded. "I'll try not to get in the way," she said.

His gaze, full of doubt, fell over her. "If you decide to go for a walk, stay away from the bull pen." He paused a half beat. "And the men's quarters."

Felicity nodded and glanced around the room. Was

there anywhere she *could* go? She smiled. "I'm glad I've got a window in my room."

He looked at her for a long moment, and a muscle twitched in his jaw. "Yeah."

The man clearly did not have a Texas-sized sense of humor. She felt an odd flutter in her stomach at the intensity in his blue eyes.

"How long are you staying?" he asked.

"I don't know. It depends on my lawyers' recommendation and what I decide. I had thought the quarters would provide some needed solitude, but..." She shrugged.

He lifted a dark eyebrow. "Your lawyers' recommendation?"

"Yes." She thought of the mess she'd left behind in New York and felt suddenly tired. "Too complicated for this hour. Thank you for your hospitality. You've truly extended yourself this evening."

He watched her for a long uncomfortable moment. "Do you have any family at all?"

Felicity felt the all-encompassing aloneness close in on her again. She stiffened herself against it. "No, but I'll be okay," she said. "I'm okay." If she kept saying it, it would one day be true.

He nodded, but didn't looked convinced. That was fine, she told herself. It was far more important that she convince herself.

She met his gaze and felt a strange undertow of recognition, as if something inside her recognized something inside him. She would almost swear she saw that same recognition in his eyes. Her heart shifted.

"Just a minute," he said, breaking the moment and

stepping into the hallway. A moment later, he returned and set bath towels and washcloths on the dresser. "If you want to take a shower, you can. The kids are asleep."

Felicity smiled and finished his thought. "So don't sing in the shower."

His lips twitched almost to a grin. "Yeah." He looked at her again, and she wondered what he saw; wondered, but wasn't sure she wanted to know.

Restless, she clasped her hands together. "Thank you for opening your home to me at such short notice."

He dipped his head. "Good night, Felicity Chambeau."

"Good night, Brock Logan."

He closed the door behind him, and she was alone again, an all-too-familiar feeling. She glanced at the bed and promised herself to sleep for twenty-four hours. She vowed not to dream about anything that would disturb her, such as a disapproving financial attorney, a cockroach former financial advisor, or a tall rancher with sexy eyes and a humor deficit.

Brock still smelled her perfume after he'd showered in the master bathroom and drunk a shot of bourbon. She wasn't exactly what he'd pictured. With a name like Felicity, he'd expected a more frivolous-looking female. Instead, her black pantsuit had whispered over her slim curves with understated ease. Her straight blond hair was pulled back into a clip at the nape of her neck. Her makeup was minimal, and he hadn't noticed any rocks on her fingers.

She'd looked like a woman who was deliberately

playing down her attributes. He frowned, wondering why. She'd almost appeared to be grieving. That wasn't possible, Brock thought, since her parents had died a few years ago. The sadness in her green eyes had tugged at him. It still did. The erotic sight of her parted lips inches away from him when she'd fallen stirred long-buried needs. Needs best denied, he thought, feeling too aware of how long he'd been without a woman.

Damn, he didn't need this. He poured another bourbon. He shouldn't have asked that last question. He'd seen the glint of pain in her gaze and her brave attempt to cover it, and in that one strange moment, he'd sensed a kindred spirit. That was impossible.

Felicity slept soundly until she heard heavy footsteps outside her door. Glancing at the clock, she winced at the afternoon hour and pulled her pillow over her head. Way too early. Not twenty-four hours. She willed herself to return to sleep.

"Sheep," she muttered, counting fluffy white animals as they jumped over a fence. She heard more heavy footsteps and pictured Brock Logan's boots. Following the image of his boots up his long legs and muscular thighs to the rest of his impressive physique, she moaned and kicked off the sheet. She tried to think of sheep, but they morphed into cows and reality began to sink in. She was not in Manhattan. She was on a cattle ranch.

"And why are you here?" she wryly asked herself. "Because you said you wanted to think about it when your financial advisor asked you to marry him."

The knowledge rubbed over her like a wire brush.

Unable to remain still one second longer, she tossed her pillow against the wall and rolled out of bed onto the floor. Her nightgown, hair and limbs in disarray, Felicity shook her head. She'd always had a little problem with her coordination.

"A robe," she murmured. Shoving her hair from her face, she scrambled to her feet and opened one suitcase, then another. She rustled through the contents until her hand encountered something hard, a picture frame. Her heart caught. Her housekeeper Anna had packed the treasured last picture taken of her and her parents.

Felicity pulled out the picture and stared instead into the weasel face of her former financial advisor, who had almost been her fiancé Doug.

Standing in the upstairs hallway with his daughter Bree, Brock heard a scream followed by a thump and shattering glass. He narrowed his gaze at the guest-bedroom door. "Go on to your room, honey," he said to Bree, nudging her down the hall.

"But something broke," she said, wide-eyed and curious despite her low-grade fever.

"I'll take care of it. You get to bed," he told her.

Brock waited until Bree went into her room then slowly opened the guest-bedroom door. "Miss Chambeau?" he began, then stopped abruptly at the sight that greeted him.

Felicity stood in the middle of the bedroom floor, her hair tousled over her shoulders and her slim curves covered by a soft satin nightie that plunged low enough to hint at the shadow of her cleavage and was short enough to reveal most of her shapely legs.

All it would take to lose the nightie would be to push the tiny straps over her shoulders. He could see the outline of her nipples. He wondered if she was totally naked beneath the garment. His mouth went dry.

Impatient with his response, he forced his gaze upward to her flushed face. Her green eyes sparked with temper, but her expression held a tinge of guilt that made him curious. He glanced at the busted picture frame.

"Miss Chambeau?" he repeated.

Felicity shrugged, drawing his gaze to her breasts. She was too feminine for his system at the moment, he thought, with resentment. Locking his gaze on her eyes, he stared at her expectantly.

"It's a picture," she said.

"Of my former financial advisor," she continued when he remained silent. "I—uh dropped—" She broke off. "I didn't expect to find *him* in my suitcase! The dirty sleazebag left the country with my money. And it's not the money. I have enough money, but I trusted him. I trusted him. I almost—" She broke off. "I can only hope he'll be eaten by a giant cockroach in the South American country where he's hiding with Chi Chi the exotic dancer and die a horrible, painful death." She finally took a breath and visibly composed herself. "But this probably isn't the best time to discuss it. I'm sorry I disturbed you."

Brock blinked at the change. There was obviously more to this story. More than he wanted to know, he emphasized to himself. "Don't move. You might cut your feet. I'll get a broom and dustpan from the linen closet." He stepped into the hallway and shook his head in disgust. This was all he needed. A kooky rich lady with a body designed to whip every male in west Texas into a state of frenzy.

Grabbing the broom and pan, he returned to find her gingerly putting shards of glass into the wastebasket. "I told you not to move."

She briefly met his gaze, then returned to her task. "My tantrum. My mess. My clean-up."

Irritation burned through him. "Listen, I've got a sick kid, and a cow ready to drop her first calf. I don't have time to take you into town for stitches."

She glanced at him with her head cocked to one side. "Oh. Who is sick?"

Brock knelt down beside her and quickly swept the glass into the dustpan. He tried not to inhale her subtle feminine scent. "My daughter Bree. I just picked her up from school. Do you want the picture?" he asked, looking at the photo of a smoothly handsome man with a weak chin.

"To burn it," she said, reaching for it.

Brock snatched it back. "Not in this room," he said, visions of a house fire filling his head. "I'll take care of it for you. More than friends, huh?"

"No, but I thought we were at least friends."

The loneliness and betrayal in her voice and eyes grabbed his gut. Brock brushed the response aside. He had no time or space for this. "I need to get my daughter to bed and get back to work."

"Thank you," she said. "How sick is she?"

"Probably just a virus, but my pediatrician brother is in Blackstone. I keep waiting for the time I reap the benefit from his medical school tuition. My house-keeper's off today, too. That calf's ready to drop. You look okay, so I'll leave,'' he muttered, and headed out the door, his mind on the three hundred pressing issues facing him.

Halfway down the hall, he heard her footsteps behind him. ''Excuse me,'' she said.

Fighting impatience, he looked over his shoulder at her. ''Yeah?''

She laced her fingers together, her prim stance at odds with her skimpy attire. ''How old is your daughter?''

''Seven. Why?'' he demanded, unable to keep the irritation from his voice

''I could stay with her,'' she offered, ''if you think that would help. I would like to help.''

Stunned, he stared at her warily. ''Wearing that?''

Felicity's cheeks bloomed with color. ''No. I'll change my clothes.'' His expression must have revealed his doubt. ''I can pour juice and water,'' she told him. ''I can read books.''

Bree would like the reading part even though she could read circles around most kids her age. For that matter, Bree might like Felicity. Brock wasn't sure that was a good idea especially since he was hoping his silent partner would be packing her impressive rear end back to New York where it belonged as soon as possible.

''You sounded busy. If you'd rather I leave her alone…''

''No,'' he said, flexing his fist in frustration. ''Thank you,'' he said, the words sounding grudging to his own ears.

She met his gaze, looking as surprised with herself as he was. The corners of her mouth lifted in a lopsided smile. "You're welcome. I'll change my clothes and be right out."

Did he really want his daughter influenced by such a woman? Brock frowned. It was just for a few hours, he told himself. The housekeeper would be back soon. Deep in his gut, however, he had a strong feeling about Felicity Chambeau. And it wasn't good. It would be easier if he could say his discomfort was due to something about her character, but he suspected it had more to do with his libido.

He swore under his breath and walked down the long hallway to Bree's room. He told his daughter Felicity would stay with her and was immediately bombarded with questions.

"Where's she from?"

"New York City," Brock said, adjusting Bree's pillow. "She's no cowgirl, but she can read to you."

"Is she old?"

"No."

"Is she pretty?"

Brock tugged at his collar. "I'll let you decide."

"But what do you think?"

Thankfully, Felicity appeared outside Bree's open door, her face scrubbed clean and her hair pulled back. She wore black jeans and a white silk shirt, but he couldn't banish the image of her in the skimpy nightie with her hair in sexy disarray.

He inhaled and drew in her teasing elusive scent. Grinding his teeth at his susceptibility, he introduced the two females, then turned to Bree. "You know my cell phone number and my pager," he told his daughter. "Call me if there's any problem."

"Cell phone, pager," Felicity echoed. "I didn't know there was cell coverage in Texas."

Brock's lips twitched, but he didn't quite smile. "We may talk slowly, but we have a few modern conveniences like running water and cell phones. What were you expecting?"

Felicity shrugged. "A bell?" she suggested.

"We have one of those, too. The cell's faster and doesn't upset everyone on the ranch." He adjusted his hat, feeling an odd twinge of discomfort at the look of curious fascination on Bree's face. "Call me if you need me, baby."

Brock left the room, and Felicity felt his departure like a physical force. Odd, she thought, that a man's absence could be so strong when his presence was so imposing. Shaking off her strange sensations, she glanced at Bree and found Brock's daughter staring back at her. Felicity felt another little twist of inadequacy. She didn't have much experience with children. She'd offered to help Brock because she could see as a single father and head of the ranch he had too much to do, and she'd added to the list by arriving last night. If she'd told him that, however, she suspected he would have died before he would ask for help, especially from her.

Okay, she might not have much experience caring for a child, but she had experience being one. Felicity returned Brock's daughter's gaze. The little girl's cheeks were slightly flushed with fever, but her blue eyes were curious and assessing.

Felicity smiled. "You have your father's eyes."

Bree smiled and nodded. "I've got his hair, too,"

she said, tugging at her long ponytail, "but you can't tell because he won't grow his long like mine."

"And you smile a little more often?" Felicity asked.

Bree nodded again. "Uncle Tyler is always telling Daddy to lighten up and he takes himself too seriously." She rolled her eyes. "My brother does that, too."

"Your brother, Jacob," Felicity clarified, immediately liking this warm, outspoken child.

"Yes ma'am. Jacob. We're twins." She cocked her head to one side thoughtfully. "You talk funny."

"It's because I'm from New York City," Felicity said.

"Oh, well you can't help it that you're not from Texas," Bree said sympathetically. "You'll be much happier now that you're here."

Felicity couldn't help chuckling. "What makes you so sure?"

"Texas is the best place in the world to live," Bree said in a matter-of-fact tone. "Everybody wants to live here," she said, then her face turned thoughtful and she rubbed her fingers over her quilt, "except my mom. She moved to California because she wants to be in the movies." She lifted her chin, another gesture that reminded Felicity of Brock. "My dad says me and Jacob are more fun than movies."

The mixture of pride and vulnerability in Bree's eyes scored her heart, reminding Felicity of the dozens of times her own mother had sought a more exciting party or exotic trip in lieu of spending time with Felicity. She thought again of Brock. An honorable man? She'd believed that species was extinct.

She met Bree's proud gaze. "You and Jacob are more fun than movies? I bet your dad is right."

"He's the best dad in the world," she said, again in the matter-of-fact voice and gave Felicity an assessing glance. "Aunt Martina says all he needs is a good woman to drive him crazy on a regular basis. We don't get many women around the Triple L. You wanna do it?"

Felicity blinked. Absolutely not, she thought, but managed a smile. "What an interesting idea. I'll have to think about it. For now, let's read a book."

Two

"There's another one ready to drop in the north pasture. I'll check on her tonight," Brock said to Chuck, his assistant foreman. His brother Tyler and son Jacob listened while they waited for Addie to put the dinner on the table. "Tomorrow, I need you to—" Brock broke off when he noticed none of them were paying attention. All three, instead, were gaping at something behind him. He frowned and turned around. "Hey, what—" Dressed in a pink sweater dress that caressed her curves the way every man would want to, Felicity Chambeau stood at the entrance to the informal dining room with a tentative expression on her face. "You said dinner is at six. May I join you?"

Her sophisticated appearance was at odds with the casual room. The oak dining-room table and chairs had served the Logans for at least three generations and bore crescent marks from teething babies, scars from forks jabbed into the surface, and though the table still gleamed, the polish wasn't as shiny as it once had been due to countless spills of milk and juice. Currently it was set with stoneware plates and bowls, stainless flatware, napkins and a pot of coffee. With her cashmere dress and golden champagne hair, Felicity clearly didn't belong here.

Brock watched Chuck suck in his gut while Tyler stepped across the room and offered his arm. "Please join us. I'm Tyler Logan. You must be Felicity Chambeau. We're delighted to have you."

Brock nearly barfed at his brother's enthusiastic greeting. "Why doesn't he just get down on his hands and knees and howl?" he muttered.

"If he doesn't, I will," Chuck said, his gaze still fastened on Felicity.

Brock exhaled in disgust. "You would think you two hadn't ever seen a woman."

"I haven't seen any that looked like her in a long time," Chuck retorted. "Just because *you're* dried up, disinterested and bitter doesn't mean the rest of us are." He stepped forward and tipped his hat. "Howdy, ma'am. I'm Chuck Granby. Pleasure to meet you."

Felicity smiled at both men, then looked at Jacob, Brock's painfully shy son. "You must be Jacob. Bree told me about you this afternoon. She said you can already rope a calf."

Jacob stuck his hands in his pockets and shrugged. "My dad taught me."

Grudgingly appreciative of her attention to his son, Brock glanced down and ruffled Jacob's hair. "Bree would speak for all of us if you gave her the chance."

"Oh, she did."

Brock could just imagine the family secrets his daughter had spilled. "Great," he muttered darkly.

"Don't worry," Felicity said. "She could easily be a PR person for the Logan family and the state of Texas. She's determined to teach me how to speak Texan."

"Maybe we can make a permanent resident of you," Tyler said with a teasing grin. "You might like it here so much you want to stay."

"Great," Brock muttered under his breath as he thought about wrapping Tyler's tongue around his throat.

His tall, sturdy housekeeper carried a steaming pot into the dining room. "Well, are y'all gonna stand around the table and look at it or sit down and eat?" She glanced up at Felicity. "You must be Miss Chambeau. I'm Addie, and I'll warn you I don't do much fancy cooking like you're probably used to in New York. Seems like these men want the same ol' thing every week or so."

Brock approved of Addie's brusque tone. She wouldn't be bowled over by a pretty woman in a pink dress.

"It smells delicious, Addie," Felicity said.

"Let me help you with your chair," Tyler smoothly said at the same time as Chuck pulled one out from the large table. After Felicity had murmured her thanks, the two men sat on either side of her like adoring bookends.

"What brings you to Texas?" Chuck asked as Addie served the beef stew.

Felicity glanced uncertainly at Brock. "I—uh—"

"She's here for a short visit," he said. He didn't want the whole crew to know she was a silent partner. He preferred that the crew not know she existed.

"She's silent partner of the Triple L," Tyler announced.

Brock fixed a glare on his brother and Tyler plastered an innocent grin on his face.

"A silent partner," Chuck echoed in amazement.

"Very silent. I'm so silent I couldn't tell the difference between a dairy cow and a steer," she emphasized as if she sensed Brock's displeasure. She was intuitive, Brock had to grant her that much. "One of my great-great-grandfathers had a little agreement with one of Mr. Logan's great-great-grandfathers. The only thing I'm entitled to is a place to sleep when I visit."

"A silent partner," Chuck murmured again, grinning from ear to ear. "A knockout from New York City, no less."

So get over it, Brock thought. He cleared his throat. "What do you do in New York?"

She hesitated. "Not as much as I would like, but I've been working on that."

"How?" Tyler asked.

She swallowed a bite and took a sip. "You'll laugh," she said to all of them. "Everyone does."

Brock took in the little signs of her discomfort, her slight wiggle in her seat, the way she dipped her head. He wondered how she managed to look appealing when she was being evasive. "I won't laugh," he said.

Her expression said she didn't believe him. She glanced at Chuck and Tyler. "I think that every person has a purpose on this earth and if you find your purpose and perform it, then you will be happy and the world will be a better place.''

Brock nodded at the philosophy. He agreed. He just would have stated it differently. ''A man's gotta do what a man's gotta do.''

Felicity's lips twitched. ''In this case, woman.''

''No argument there,'' Chuck murmured.

''I'm in an unusual position,'' Felicity continued. ''My family has a history of being fortunate with their investments.''

''She's loaded, too?'' Chuck asked.

Tyler muffled a chuckle.

''Cut it,'' Brock said.

Chuck stuffed a bite of stew in his mouth.

''Now that my parents are gone, I have to make decisions,'' she said, sadness clouding her eyes. ''My family has been fairly generous with charitable causes, but I think it's my purpose to take that charity a step further.''

''In what way?'' Tyler asked, no more curious than Brock was.

''I want to give away a significant portion of my inheritance,'' she said. ''I want to give the money to a worthy cause.''

Silence followed, and all three men stared at Felicity as if she'd spoken in Swahili.

Brock stifled a sigh. God save him from crazy women with more money than sense.

She gave a low chuckle. ''Well, you didn't laugh, but you look just like my financial advisors did the first time I told them what I wanted to do. I'm not clinically insane,'' she assured them.

''Why don't you want to keep it?'' Chuck asked.

Brock watched the world-weariness tug at her wry smile. "Because the only thing the money is doing right now is accumulating. For what? There are better uses for it."

"If you need a worthy cause," Tyler said, "the hospital where I practice needs—"

"—Tyler," Brock interrupted before his brother could get too wound up.

"If she wants to donate it to a worthy cause, we could use—"

"Miss Chambeau is a guest in our house. We don't badger guests for money," he said in the quiet, but rock-hard voice he used when he pulled rank. "Even for good causes."

Tyler sighed impatiently, but dug into his stew.

Chuck shook his head. "I never heard of that one. So your job is to give away your money. Why don't you want to keep it for your husband and kids?"

"I don't have a husband and children," she said in a crisp voice.

"Yeah, but some lucky guy'll get a ring on your finger—"

Felicity shook her head. "I'm not getting married. Right now, my appeal to men is my inheritance. As soon as I give half of it away, my appeal will disappear."

Half of it! Her statement was like another little bomb exploding. Brock stared at her in silence. Surely the woman knew she possessed more attractions than her endless supply of dead presidents.

Tyler cleared his throat. "You might bump into someone who can change your mind about that," he said in a mild voice that bordered on flirtatious.

Felicity appeared to ignore the hint of flattery and firmly shook her head.

Chuck wrinkled his brow. "I still don't get what you're doing down here."

"She's down here so she can get away from the city and think without being questioned half to death," Brock said, thinking the woman clearly needed a keeper. He was in no way interested in the job, but he wasn't going to let anyone take advantage of her while she was in his house. The light was beginning to dawn. Her lawyers had probably sent her down here until she cooled on the idea of ditching her fortune. So now she was *his* problem.

"Oh," Chuck said. "Well, after dinner if you'd like a tour around the ranch I'll be glad to—"

"We've got that heifer ready to drop in the north pasture," Brock said.

"I thought you were going to check on that one."

"I'm doing the late check tonight. If Miss Chambeau wants to look at the ranch, I'll take her." He glanced up at Felicity.

"That would be nice. I haven't been out today," Felicity said, surprise widening her eyes. "Thank you."

For the rest of the meal, Tyler took over the conversation and shared a humorous account about one of his young patients. They discussed Bree's virus. Brock glanced at Felicity. Her breeding showed in her impeccable manners, but there was an empathy in her that he wouldn't have expected. He noticed she gave the person to whom she was speaking her undivided attention, and lit up the table with her smile. She was no hardship to watch. The men would soon learn that fact. It wouldn't be long before the whole county knew it. She was going to be one hell of a hardship to keep at the ranch, he thought, grinding his teeth.

Brock noticed his son's quiet curious gaze on her through most of the meal. He wondered how much Jacob missed having a mother, and felt a hollowness in the pit of his stomach. He didn't have to worry with Bree. She made her preferences and needs known loud and clear. Jacob, however, felt things deeply and kept his thoughts to himself. Lately, in fact, he'd seemed a little too quiet.

When Addie brought cherry pie to the table, Felicity lifted her hand to refuse, then slid a glance to Jacob. "The stew was so good I can only eat a couple of bites of pie. Do you think you could help me?"

Jacob eagerly nodded. "Yes ma'am."

Brock narrowed his eyes. His brother was intrigued with Felicity, and Chuck was salivating. His son was immune, though, he was sure of it. The ominous feeling in his gut tightened, however. If he didn't keep a tight rein on her, Felicity Chambeau was going to wreak havoc at the Triple L.

After Brock checked on Bree, Felicity followed him out into the cool night air. She had readily agreed when he'd suggested a walk instead of a full tour. They wandered along the path beside the fence, and she took in her surroundings as well as she could, considering the darkness. She glanced up. The sky was huge and full of stars. Although she knew her ancestors, along with her parents, were turning in their graves, announcing her intentions had been liberating.

She noticed the silence again. "It's so quiet it feels loud," she said, shaking her head.

"You're just not used to it. If you listen you'll hear the rustle of tree leaves in the breeze or a mockingbird. A little farther down the drive, you might hear a cow."

Felicity stood still and closed her eyes. She heard the rustle of tree leaves. It was a fresh, musical sound that made her fingers itch to play the piano.

"Do you make a habit of telling people you're going to give away half of your fortune?" he asked, interrupting the magical moment.

She opened her eyes and met Brock's gaze. His intensity made her nervous, but she didn't blink. "I thought you would laugh, and I knew you would think I'm crazy."

"I just wondered if that was the reason your attorneys sent you down here."

She sighed and walked over to the wooden fence. The wood was rough to her touch. "They're hoping I'll change my mind."

"If you tell everyone you meet that you're going to give away your money, then a lot of people will try to take advantage of you. Your attorneys are probably trying to protect you."

"My attorneys have dollar signs in their eyes. Besides, I haven't told everyone my plans. In New York, I confided in Douglas, and it turns out that was a very poor choice. And my attorneys are *not* trying to protect me," she insisted. "They're appalled that I'm considering doing such a thing and hoping I will change my mind."

"Why do you think you won't ever get married?" he demanded, then shrugged. "You're not ugly."

Felicity gave a double take at his pseudo-compliment. "Your absence of flattery is refreshing. Orthodontics is primitive, but you can't deny the results," she said, baring her teeth. "The contact lenses do their job, the physical trainer has done his, and the makeup artist at Georgette Klinger beauty salon has shared a few of her tricks with me. A lasting relationship means someone would love me for who I am on the inside. The Chambeaus have a history of developing their fortune, not their inner selves. I don't want the kind of marriage my parents had, and I'm not sure I would know how to make anything better, so maybe I'd just better work on making the world and me better."

Felicity took in the long-suffering expression on Brock's face and gave a wry smile. "I think I was saying that more to me than to you. You're an innocent passerby who got hit by my incoming lecture. I'm sorry."

He shrugged. "You just sound kinda like Tyler did when he was thinking about being a psychiatrist. Thank God that phase didn't last long."

Felicity laughed. "Too much self-examination—"

"—is a waste of time and depressing. Not only that," Brock said, "it causes indigestion. You need to find a job or get married. If you get busy, you'll feel better."

"I'm not getting married," Felicity insisted. "And my primary skill has been writing checks to lawyers, financial consultants, and charities my mother favored."

Impatience tightened his mouth. "Well, while you're here I'd appreciate it if you wouldn't tell everyone you meet that you're planning to give away half your fortune. We're not set up to deal with the influx of traffic at the Triple L, especially during calving season.''

"You think I'm nuts. Go ahead and admit it," she dared him. "You think I'm teetotally crazy," she said, choosing an expression she'd heard Bree use.

"You're not thinking about your heritage—" he began.

"I have no heritage," she said. "I refuse to have the same kind of marriage my parents had. They led separate lives, and I was a disappointment to them. I was a clumsy, shy little girl with crooked teeth who liked to read a lot. I played the piano, but not quite well enough to be a concert pianist. I made good grades, but I wasn't gifted. And socially, I didn't *sparkle*." She straightened her shoulders. "Sharing my wealth is the one way I can make my mark, the one way I can do something good and productive."

Brock sighed and squeezed the bridge of his nose as if he had a headache. "I didn't want to ask this," he muttered. "Why are you down here?"

"I told you. My lawyers—"

"Why did they send you to me?"

"It wasn't specifically to you," she told him. All the same, she thought, his broad shoulders could handle anything.

"It was specifically to get you out of their hair for a while. Why did they send you away?"

"Because I hired a financial consultant to help me set up a foundation."

"Douglas," Brock said.

Regret and anger roiled through her. Felicity

frowned. "Yes. Doug. He once worked for the firm my father used. I met him at a social function, and he told me he'd gone into business for himself. He called me a few times and appeared genuinely interested in helping me. I began to transfer funds for the foundation. Three weeks ago, he took that money and left for South America. My attorneys don't trust my judgment. At the moment, I don't trust myself either. I need someone I can trust. Someone who isn't interested in me. Someone with integrity," she said, looking at him thoughtfully.

"After you dump your money, what will you do?" Brock asked.

Felicity shrugged. She had only a vague picture of her future. "I don't know. Enter a convent or buy a cottage on the coast of Maine and read and have three cats. I'm not sure it's all that important. What's important is that I set up this foundation."

"They're not going to let you in a convent with your body," Brock muttered.

Her stomach took a little dip. She ignored it. "Then Maine it is," she said wryly, then turned serious. "Would you help me?"

He shot her a wary look. "You just met me. Why would you trust me?"

"Several reasons. Gut feeling." She wouldn't tell him she had an odd sense of fate about Brock. Nothing romantic, of course. He was trustworthy. "You're solid and responsible. You give the impression that you were born forty years old. You come highly recommended," she said. "Your daughter says you're the best. You kept your end of a bargain you didn't make by letting me stay in your home. Plus there are the other reasons.''

''And they are?'' he prompted in a skeptical tone.

''You don't like me. You don't want me here. In fact,'' she said, pushing aside her little twinge, ''you don't want me, period.''

Three

God save him from the female gender, Brock thought, and shook his head. "I said you weren't ugly," he told her.

"There's a large gap between not ugly and attractive," Felicity said with a Mona Lisa smile.

She hugged her arms against the cold and Brock couldn't help noticing the way her nipples beaded against her sweater dress. It was easy to imagine how her breasts would look and feel naked; rounded ivory mounds with small raspberry tips, soft, sensitive, responsive. She would feel like heaven in his hands, against his chest, in his mouth.

And there would be hell to pay, he thought as he remembered Felicity was the proverbial Ms. Moneybags.

"You're an honorable man," she said, meeting his

gaze. "I thought honor was an extinct virtue among men, but you possess it. I think you could help me."

Brock sighed. He didn't spend much time thinking about honor and virtue. He just tried to do what was right. "What do you want from me? I'm no lawyer."

"You can help me find someone I can trust to set up the foundation. I can tell you're not a man to be taken advantage of. I don't seem to have developed that skill yet," she said wryly.

Everything she said was true, but Brock still didn't feel right helping Felicity part with half her fortune. "How old are you?"

"Twenty-four," she said. "Why is that important?"

"I'd feel easier about this if you were about sixty years older, if you'd lived more and longer and had more experience."

"Maybe you could pretend," she said with a cheeky smile.

He eyed her body once more and shook his head. "Not likely," he said dryly. "You've never been married or had any children," he repeated.

"Neither," she said.

"Getting married and having children might change your perspective," he told her.

"I already told you I'm not doing that."

"You could change your mind."

"I can't. It's not meant to be. I accept that. My purpose is to do something else," she said earnestly and stepped closer to him. "I may not be older, more experienced or married, but I can identify need. I want to do something about it. There's an emptiness in me, and I know the only way I can make it go away is to do this. Is it so bad that I want to make life better for some people? Is it so bad that I don't want to hoard what I have? That I want to share it instead?''

Her passion and vulnerability tugged at his heart. For someone with so much, she understood the fulfillment in giving. Brock was torn. On one hand, it went against every drop of his Logan blood for Felicity to insist that she was unconcerned about the heritage of her future family. On the other hand, he could see that she was trying to create a different kind of heritage. "Okay, duchess, just for this moment, let's say I help you give away your money. What are you going to do with the rest of your life?''

"I don't know. That's not what is important—" she began.

"That's where I disagree. This is a mighty big decision, and you have the rest of your life to live with it. And I have the rest of my life to live with aiding and abetting your..." he paused, then finished his thought, "...your insanity or generosity.''

"But—"

"But nothing," he said, adjusting his hat. "I want you to think about this for a couple of weeks and tell me what you have planned for yourself, how you're going to live your life. Then, we'll see.''

Felicity didn't want to wait. Her goal burned like a coal in her gut. Since Doug had left the country with her money, she'd felt as if she'd taken ten steps backward. "It's called exploring your options.'' Brock leaned closer. "I can tell you're trying to find a way around what I'm saying, but if you want my integrity, honor and help, then you're gonna have to do this my way. I have a bad feeling that if I don't take the reins

when you and I go down this road together, then I'll
end up in the ditch.''

Although Brock could tell she wanted to argue,
some remnant of sanity must have made her hold her
tongue. After he escorted Ms. Moneybags back to the
house, he took the truck out to make a late-night check
on the cow. She hadn't dropped. It could happen tomorrow or the next day. One of his neighbor's bulls
had waded through a shared stream and had a field
day with his cows. That could mess up the birth weight
of the calves, so he had to watch carefully. The
weather was still iffy at night. Cattle weren't the most
intelligent animals on the earth and he'd watched a
few new moms drop their babies in freezing water.
After Felicity had disrupted his evening, he needed
some time to himself to clear his head. He took in the
wide starry sky and gradually began to feel a glimmer
of peace return.

Brock looked out at the north pasture and knew he
was where he was supposed to be. The uncomfortable
thought struck him, however, that Felicity had no idea
where she belonged.

He got into the truck and rode back to the house.
He turned out the lights and carefully locked the doors.
Since his dad got sick, it had been his job to lock up
for the night and make sure the Logans were safe. He
climbed the stairs and peeked in on his daughter and
son, then went to his room and shut his door.

After his shower, he stood, nude, in the dark inside
his bedroom. He had systematically closed and locked
the doors to his house to protect his family. During
the last several years, he had systematically closed
himself off to his needs. He didn't want to feel. He

didn't want another woman swinging a wrecking ball through his guts. He'd almost convinced himself and everyone he knew that he didn't *have* needs anymore.

As he stood alone in his room, however, he remembered the combination of softness and fire in Felicity's eyes, her stubborn intention to rid herself of her wealth, and, most disconcerting, her belief in him, his character, his integrity.

He remembered her sweet scent and sweeter curves. He'd been bred for honor. She was right about that. But when she'd insisted he wasn't attracted to her and didn't want her, the woman was dead wrong.

Even now, though he hadn't touched her, his body was hard with wanting, with the need to mold her to him and take her, to taste her and take her again. He was alarmingly susceptible to her. A half-hearted flirting remark sent his hormones pumping through his blood like an oil gusher.

It was raging desire. It was raging insanity.

He closed his eyes to the unfamiliar sensations coursing through him and mentally snapped his walls into place. He would not have her. Just as Felicity had concluded she wouldn't love a man because of the curse of her wealth, Brock knew he would never risk loving another woman because of the Logan Curse. Logans never won at love.

"I'm bored," Bree said after Felicity finished reading the third book the next morning. The little girl rolled her head from side to side on her pillow. Finding ways to keep Bree occupied was far easier than trying to figure out what to do with the rest of her life. Brock Logan, she'd decided, was honest, honorable and impossible. She rolled her eyes at the assignment he'd given her, then banished it from her mind.

"You must be feeling better," Felicity said as she searched for another way to entertain Brock's daughter. She thought back to her own childhood and smiled. "But just to be sure, I think I'm going to give you Marybel's cure."

"Who's Marybel?" Bree stopped moving her head and looked at Felicity curiously.

"She was my very favorite nanny," Felicity told her, fondly remembering the one person in her life who had made her feel adored. Marybel had applauded when Felicity played "Chopsticks" on the piano and had told her what a pretty girl she was when Felicity wore braces and glasses. When Felicity was sent to boarding school, Marybel had left. She still missed the woman.

"What kind of cure?" Bree demanded.

"Wait right there," she told her.

"Texans say hold your horses," Bree corrected.

Felicity chuckled at Bree's attempts to Texanize her and waved her hand. "Okay, hold your horses or cows," she said.

"Cattle," Bree corrected again.

"Exactly," Felicity agreed and went to the guest room to get a few items from her cosmetic case. Returning to Bree's room, she lined up five bottles of nail polish on the girl's bed. "Choose one."

Bree sat up and brightened at the sight of the different colors. "This is the cure?"

"*Mani*cure, or as Marybel used to say, cure for whatever ails you."

"I never heard of that."

Felicity saw her father's skepticism creep into Bree's eyes. "Then it's time you did. Whether you're heartsick or body-sick, a cure just helps you feel better." Felicity thought about her recent disaster with Douglas. "Although if there's a man involved, you might need a day at the spa. Choose one," Felicity said again.

Bree frowned. "Do I have to pick just one?"

Felicity started to nod, then stopped mid-motion, remembering part of the fun of the cure when she'd been a child was that she'd been allowed to choose and whatever she had chosen was fine with Marybel. "No, you can have all five if you like."

Bree gave a slow smile. "That's what I want."

Felicity proceeded to create a rainbow on Bree's fingernails and toenails. By the time she'd finished Bree was beaming. "Wow. I can't wait for Dad to see this."

Felicity swallowed a secret chuckle. "Me either."

"Have you decided if you can drive him crazy?" Bree asked.

"Oh, I think we're probably driving each other a little crazy," she said. "I asked your father to help me with something, but he wants me to do something first."

"He always does that," Bree said. "If I ask for help with my homework, he says I have to try first myself. Do you have homework?"

"In a way," Felicity muttered. "I think I need a book. Do you know of any bookstores nearby?"

"There's one in town," Bree told her, admiring her fingernails and wiggling her toes when Felicity bent down to blow on them.

"How do you get there?"

"With Daddy or Addie. One of the hands usually makes a trip to town for something every day or so."

"Okay," Felicity said, formulating a plan as she watched Bree yawn for the third time. "It's time for you to rest, so you need to get those tootsies under the covers. I painted them first, so they would be nice and dry."

Bree didn't protest, which proved she was tired. "What are we going to do this afternoon?" she asked.

"I don't know, yet. I may go out while you rest, but Addie will be here if you need her."

Felicity pulled the covers up and brushed Bree's hair from her face. Her heart gave an odd turn at the knowledge that Bree's mother had left her and Jacob. Felicity knew she would never be a mother or anything permanent to Bree, but she couldn't help remembering all the things she'd longed for from her mother. She might not be a permanent force in Bree's life, but Felicity hoped she could be a positive one. She kissed Bree's forehead, "Go to sleep, so the cure will work."

Bree sighed and caught Felicity off guard when she pursed her lips to kiss her on the cheek. "You'll come back this afternoon, won't you?" Bree asked.

Felicity felt her insides tighten. "Sure, I will."

Brock checked his watch and took off his hat to cool his head for a moment. He'd been going non-stop since he'd risen this morning. A busted fence had earned him sharp words from his long-time neighbors the Coltranes when some of his cattle travelled off Logan land.

The new hand, Ray, should be back from town any

minute with veterinary supplies. As soon as the thought graced Brock's mind, he spied a truck whizzing down the lane. Ray barely slowed as he passed the barn, calling out, "Be right back."

Brock saw Felicity wave from the passenger seat before the truck headed toward the house. Brock narrowed his eyes and a slow burn began to spread through his blood. He'd told her to stay away from the men's quarters. He'd known the woman was trouble, known it before he even laid eyes on her.

Ray pulled the truck next to the barn in no time and got out and began to unload. "Hey, Mr. Logan. Got the supplies."

Brock bit the inside of his cheek to check his anger. "What did Miss Chambeau want?"

"Oh, Flip?" Ray asked. "She just wanted a ride to the bookstore."

"Flip?" Brock repeated.

"Yeah, she said that was a nickname one of her nannies gave her." He shook his head. "That's one pretty nice lady. If she needs someone to drive her anywhere or service her in any way," he said with a sly grin, "I'm her man."

Brock's internal temperature soared. "It's not your job to chauffeur Miss Chambeau. If you don't have enough to do, we're at the beginning of calving season and there will be plenty to do."

Ray looked taken aback. "Hey, I was just offering. The lady doesn't have a driver's license since she's always lived in the city. That's why she asked for a ride today. I kept my hands off of her, but I wouldn't mind putting them on her. She's the sweetest piece of—"

"Keep your mind on the job, Ray," Brock cut in and carried another bag into the barn.

Ray opened his mouth to respond, then, seeming to change his mind, he wisely kept silent. After they'd finished unloading, Brock drove to the north pasture. He would deal with Felicity later.

Hours later when Brock walked through the front door of the house, the first thing he heard was the sound of piano music echoing from the back room. A curious wave of melancholy and sweet nostalgia rolled through him. The Steinway baby grand had not been played in over twenty years, not since his sister Martina had been born, and his mother had died.

The person with the easy expressive touch on the ivories clearly knew how to play. Felicity. Brock sighed and walked toward the back room, the large library which had been his father's domain.

He hesitated before entering. The dark room was rarely used. Felicity played another measure and several keys twanged out of tune. She stopped.

"This is hideous," she muttered, then doggedly continued with the piece.

Brock stepped into the room, taken aback at the sight that greeted him. The heavy drapes that usually shielded the windows lay in heaps on the floor with the brass rods underneath. The late evening sun shone on the dust in the air.

The whole room was probably in shock as much from exposure to the sun as the broken silence. Wearing a hot-pink silk blouse and a long black skirt, Felicity sat erect on the wooden bench, her stocking-clad foot arched against the brass pedal. His gaze was drawn to her pink toenails, the sight feminine and sexy. While he listened to the sound of a fast-moving melodic tune, he looked her up and down.

She was Queen of Chaos.

More twangy notes sounded.

Her back to him, Felicity swore under her breath, then growled and played more loudly. She finished the piece and stopped. The silence was deafening.

"It hasn't been tuned in over twenty years," Brock told her.

She turned around and met his gaze. "That recently," she said irritably. "I wasn't sure if someone had touched it since the turn of the century."

His lips twitched. She was a snob about sound. "My father bought the piano for my mother. She played it," he told her. "She died when Martina was born."

Her eyes turned thoughtful. "Oh, I'm sorry." She glanced around the room. "Have I desecrated hallowed ground?"

"Yes," Brock said.

She looked at him again. "You don't seem offended."

"Other fish to fry," he told her. "I told you to stay away from the men's quarters."

"I stayed away from the men's quarters. I visited the barn."

He raised an eyebrow. "Splitting hairs?"

"Did you say the barn was off limits?"

"No," he admitted grudgingly.

"I didn't want to ask Addie to take me to town because you specifically told me not to burden her. Bree told me one of the hands usually goes into town, so I asked for a ride."

"I don't want you distracting the men," Brock began.

"I didn't distract Ray," Felicity said, impatience cutting into her voice. "He dropped me off at the bookstore while he went to the feed store."

"You distracted him," Brock corrected her. "He let me know he'd like to do more than drive you to town."

Felicity rolled her eyes and waved her hand in a dismissing gesture. "It doesn't mean anything."

"I can't have you distracting the men during calving season," Brock told her.

"I don't think there's any threat of an insurrection," Felicity said dryly.

"The next time you want to go to town, you either go with Addie or me," he instructed.

Felicity stood up from the black piano bench. "With all due respect, I think you're being ridiculous. It's not as if I gave in to an urge to go up on the roof and sunbathe topless."

The sensual image of her bare breasts was one more jolt on a day when he felt as if he might as well have been riding a bronc. "When did you forget you're a silent partner?"

"When you stopped being reasonable. Honestly, Brock, you gave me an assignment. How in the world am I supposed to do what you asked me to do if I don't get out?" She picked up two books from the piano. "Occupational assessment and aptitude. I did the skills inventory and have learned I might be able to get a job in a bar. I play the piano and know how to mix drinks."

"I'm sure you have other talents and abilities,"

Brock said. Unfortunately, the talents and abilities that filled his mind showed Felicity naked and in his bed. Never-ever land, cowboy, he told himself.

"I don't understand why you're insisting that I plan my future. You believe that giving away part of my inheritance to a worthy cause is good. I can see it. I can feel it."

Not for the first time, Brock wished Felicity wasn't so intuitive. "You're only solving part of the problem. You feel useless and you think donating your money will give you fulfillment, but what you want is to create a heritage. That's going to take more than plopping down a few million. Maybe you should look into managing the trust yourself."

"There are a zillion laws and provisions," she said.

He stepped closer and stroked his finger down a strand of her hair. "Use what's under this pretty blond hair."

Her eyes met his and he felt a kick inside him that would rival a ride on an unbroken stud. Her gaze darkened and for a fraction of a second, he wondered if she felt it, too.

He watched her throat work with a swallow. "The pretty blond hair is courtesy of a bottle."

He wondered why she continued to play down her appeal. "Maybe," he said, then skimmed his thumb over her cheek and down to her mouth "but you've got a lot that didn't come from a bottle."

"If you're not careful," Felicity whispered, "you're going to give the impossible and false impression that you're attracted to me."

He stared at her lips. "I said you weren't ugly," he muttered, probing just past her lips with his thumb.

She took a quick shallow breath. "You can't kiss me."

"Why not?" he asked, skimming his hand down her throat, then dropping it to his side.

"Because you're an honorable man."

Here we go again. "If I'm such an honorable man, I can't let you keep thinking you're not attractive."

"Sure you can," she said nervously.

Brock shook his head and lowered his mouth

"You don't like me," she reminded him in a voice that bordered on desperate. She seemed trapped, yet he wasn't touching her. "You don't want me here. Remember? You think I'm a pain in the butt. Besides," she added, "Bree said she wanted to see you."

Brock stopped at the mention of his daughter's name. "Is she worse?"

Felicity took a breath and stumbled backward. "No, she's much better, but she said she wanted to see you." She cleared her throat and lifted her lips in a smile that worried him. "She wants to show you something."

He glanced at her again. "What's that?"

She smiled again, more broadly. "I promised not to tell."

Uh-oh, Brock thought, feeling a sinking sensation in his gut. "Then I'll go see her now."

He felt Felicity's gaze on him as he walked toward the doorway. "Do you ever tell her how pretty and smart she is?"

The question turned him around. "I tell her she's the prettiest, smartest and best daughter a man could have, because she is."

"Good," she said in a soft voice.

He saw a dozen powerful emotions flash in her eyes as she nodded. For just a moment, he pictured her as a little girl needing to hear someone tell her she was pretty or smart. From the look in her gaze, she hadn't heard it. He felt a weird unexpected twist of sadness and an urge to protect, while at the same time he burned to take her, all of which proved the woman could cause chaos inside as well as out.

Brock left her with a warning. "Felicity, telling a Logan he can't do something is a surefire invitation for him to prove he can."

Felicity locked her knees and held her breath until the sound of his footsteps disappeared. Then she sank onto the piano bench.

Her hands were trembling. Her insides were trembling. He had almost kissed her and she was a wreck. Heaven help her, what if he had really kissed her?

Felicity closed her eyes. She had wanted him to kiss her at the same time as she'd feared it. She touched her fingers to her lips and cheek, where his calloused hand had been. Was his mouth as hard as it looked? How would he taste? How would she feel in his arms?

Felicity's internal alarm system clanged in warning. She could want Brock. Worse yet, she could like him. She could like him for being an honorable man. She could like him for giving his daughter what Felicity had never received as a child. The combination of want and like was dangerous. She'd never experienced it before.

He didn't want her on the ranch. He viewed her as an inconvenience, which she technically was. But the fire in his eyes when he'd looked at her just moments ago rocked her from her head to her toes and every secret place in between.

He induced an odd range of emotions. She sensed she could trust him, and at the same time she wanted more than a glimpse of the passion she'd seen.

In another situation, she might let her curiosity get the best of her. He didn't want her money. In fact, she'd bet he would tell her to leave if not for his sense of honor and upbringing. What would Brock Logan be like if he shed all that self-control? With her. Her mind was filled with the image of his strong body, persuasive, practiced hands, and his voice, deep with pleasure.

Felicity felt her nipples bead against her blouse and a sensual ache between her thighs. Surprised at her response, she took a deep breath and stood.

The important point for her to remember was that although Brock might want her, he didn't like her.

Four

————

"Can't stand the rain," Addie muttered as she brought a plate of hamburgers and a pot of beans into the dining room. "It makes my arthritis act up."

"Can I help serve the drinks?" Felicity offered.

"I already fixed iced tea for you and milk for the kids. Bree, have you seen your brother?"

"Not since we got home from school," Bree said. "My class got our interim reports today, but Jacob's didn't. I got all As," she said proudly.

Felicity smiled, remembering how Bree had run past her snack to share the news with her. She had been terribly impressed and Bree had beamed with pleasure.

"Good for you," Addie said. "When I get a hold of your brother, he'll never be late for dinner again. Y'all go ahead and start."

She walked out of the room to the edge of the stairs

and bellowed. "Jacob Logan, your dinner is ready now!"

Felicity exchanged a look with Bree.

"She always gets cranky when her arthritis bothers her," Bree whispered.

Felicity nodded. "Where is Jacob?"

"I dunno. He doesn't miss dinner unless he's out roping or riding with Dad."

"But your father is at the Cattleman Association's meeting and it's raining."

Bree shrugged and reached for a hamburger. Addie returned to the room, fuming.

Felicity felt a trickle of concern. It was dark, cold and rainy outside. Jacob may have grown up on the ranch, but he was still young. "When did you last see Jacob?"

"When he walked in the door from school. He's never noisy, but he didn't say a word today. Just went straight to his room. Come to think of it, he didn't eat his snack." Addie frowned. "I wonder if that rounder is sick."

Felicity stood. "I'll check his room. Save your knees," she said and dashed upstairs. His room was neat except for the books and notebooks spilled onto the middle of the floor. There was no sign of Jacob. She bent over to straighten the books and a folder of graded papers spilled out. She saw an F on an English paper, then another, a C and an A on Math. Feeling as if she were intruding, she quickly shuffled the papers together, put them in the folder, and went downstairs.

"He wasn't there."

"I'm getting worried about that boy," Addie said. "He never misses a meal."

"Does this mean I can have his dessert?" Bree asked with sibling devotion.

"You concentrate on your dinner, missy. Dessert tonight is a banana," Addie said.

Bree made a face that would have made Felicity chuckle if she hadn't been concerned about Jacob. "Maybe I should check a few places outside. Is there anywhere he especially likes to go?"

"One of the barns," Bree said, after she swallowed another bite of burger.

"His daddy taught him better than this," Addie grumbled in a worried voice. "That boy should have enough sense to come out of the rain. If he doesn't get home soon, his daddy will have him mucking out stalls until he turns eighteen."

A fate worse than death as far as Felicity was concerned. She wrinkled her nose. "Let me get my raincoat."

A few minutes later, she donned her Dior raincoat, impulsively grabbed a hat sitting on the foyer table and tramped down the drive. Although Felicity knew she wasn't particularly good with children, she hoped she could find Jacob and save him from, well, a lot of muck.

From Bree and Addie, she'd learned the Triple L had several barns. She tried the one she'd visited the other day and didn't find him, so she turned around and headed for the horse barn.

By the time she sloshed her way to the wooden structure, her feet were drenched and the rest of her was damp. Dior apparently hadn't spent much time in a Texas downpour.

Felicity pushed open the door and waited for her eyes to adjust to the darkness. She inhaled the scents of fresh hay and horseflesh. She checked the tack room and a closet, then the stalls. In the corner of the last stall, she spotted Jacob, his arms tucked around him and his hat shielding his face.

"Go away!" he yelled.

Felicity might have, but she heard misery behind the anger in his voice that tugged at her. At a loss, she ducked her head and sighed. Now that she'd found Jacob, she had no clue what to do. Right now, she wished she had taken a child psychology course or two in college.

"I said go away!"

"I can't do that," she said. "When you didn't show for dinner Addie and I became worried. She said your father would be very upset, so I'm here to keep you from a lifetime of mucking out stalls."

"I'm already gonna be grounded as soon as Dad finds out about my grades," he said in a low voice. "I can't read worth a cow paddy. A stupid ol' cow's smarter than I am."

Felicity unlatched the stall door and entered, searching for the right words. "I can't imagine a cow being smarter than you," she said. "Have you ever been roped by a cow?"

"No, but—"

"Didn't I hear that you could rope a calf a couple of years ago?"

"Yeah," he said grudgingly. "Okay, I might be a

little smarter than a dumb cow, but that's not saying much. Even my dad says cattle are dumb.''

"I bet you know some things I don't know," Felicity said. "Do you know how to take care of a horse?''

"Yeah. So?''

"So, stop calling yourself dumb because you're having a little trouble with reading. Einstein had problems reading when he was young, too.''

Jacob's head whipped up. "He did?''

"Yes. His teachers said he wouldn't amount to anything. Look how wrong they were.''

For a long moment, Jacob met her gaze with eyes red from tears. She saw a glimmer of hope, then he rubbed his nose with his sleeve.

"My dad is gonna kill me when he sees my grades.''

"He's not going to kill you," she said. "He loves you too much to kill you.''

"You don't understand. My dad is an Aggie. He went on a football scholarship and graduated with honors. He expects the same from me.''

Aggie, football, honors. Felicity tried to put it all together. "An Aggie?''

"Yeah. A graduate of Texas A&M, the best university in the country," Jacob said.

Felicity's lips twitched, but she managed to bite back a grin. "A few people from Harvard might argue with that, but what does that have to do with you?''

"He's smart. He can do anything. I want to be like that.''

"You are like him in many ways," Felicity said.

"But you don't have to send in your application for Texas M—"

"Texas A&M," Jacob corrected.

"Right," Felicity said. "You don't have to send in your application for a few more years."

"I'm gonna flunk second grade."

"You're not going to flunk second grade. You're very smart," she told him. "You know what you are. You're brilliant. You just need a little help. I'll help you," she said impulsively, hoping she could.

At that moment, Brock Logan pushed open the barn door and strode to the back of the barn.

Felicity's heart sank. She stared at Jacob.

"Now, we're both gonna be mucking out stalls," Jacob whispered.

Felicity gave a double take. "Why me?"

"'Cause my dad has two favorite hats, and you're wearing one of them."

Brock looked in the open stall and his gaze landed on Felicity with his son. They were okay. Brock felt a gush of sweet relief and savored the moment. Jacob was okay. Felicity was okay.

Both of their faces were shadowed with guilt. On the heels of relief, anger punched in. What was Felicity trying to do? He noticed his hat on her head and felt a stab of irritation. The hat was bad enough, but Brock didn't want Felicity interfering with his son. She had gone too far.

Felicity fluttered to her feet. "Brock, I—you—"

Brock held up his hand, not trusting himself to hear any lame explanations. "It's late and raining," he said. "Let's get home."

"But I want you to—"

"Not now," he said. "Jacob should be in bed."

When Jacob scrambled to his feet Felicity gave his son's shoulder a reassuring squeeze. The gesture tugged at him and irritated him at the same time. Brock waited for the two of them to step in front of him. They trudged outside and Felicity quickly whipped around, nearly catching him by surprise.

She pulled the hat off and pressed it into his hands. "Here. I'm sorry," she said, and whirled away.

Brock strode behind her, idly noticing that she had ruined the creases in his Stetson. The hat had fit perfectly, looked perfect, and he'd paid a pretty penny for it.

He glanced at her bare head dampened by the rain and sighed. Expanding his stride, he reached forward and returned the hat to her head. "It's raining. You need the protection."

Her wide wary green eyes met his. "But it's your favorite hat."

He chuckled wryly. "It *was*. Get the lead out."

Still wary, she hurried along. As soon as they arrived at the house, he hustled Jacob up to his room. "Do you have something you need to tell me?"

Jacob's jaw tightened. "Not now," he muttered.

Brock wanted to pick the boy up by his toes and shake his secrets from him, but he also wanted Jacob willing to share. "Then I'll look forward to your explanation tomorrow," he said. "Brush your teeth and get to bed."

After Jacob tugged on his pajamas and brushed his teeth, Brock hugged his son. "You got a lot of people worried and upset tonight."

"I'm sorry, Dad," Jacob said miserably.

"Don't do it again. G'night."

Brock tucked the covers around Jacob, then left the room. He glanced down the hallway and saw Felicity standing outside her door. "Is he okay?" she asked.

Brock felt a scrape of irritation and strode toward her. "He'll be fine. It's not your concern."

Felicity looked taken aback. "Well, of course I was concerned when he was missing from dinner."

"He's not your son. He's not anything to you."

"I know he's not my son, but he's a human being. I still care about him."

His frustration reaching a new high, he pulled Felicity into her room and closed the door. "I don't want you intruding with my kids. You're not going to be here very long and I don't want them getting attached. Jacob doesn't need you to care about him. He'll be just fine without you. In fact, he'll be better off."

Felicity stared at him, blinking. She appeared to hold her breath so long Brock wondered if he should remind her to breathe.

Pain slashed through her eyes, and she finally took a quick little breath. "I was trying to help. Addie's arthritis was bothering her and you were gone and—"

Brock didn't want to hear it. "Just stay out of it."

"—and since Jacob is having problems with reading," she said, her voice distressed, "and it's breeding season—"

"Calving season," Brock automatically corrected, feeling as if he'd just been punched. "Jacob's having problems with reading?"

Felicity slowly nodded. "Since you're busy with

calving season, I thought I could help him in the afternoons after school.''

He turned away and raked his hand through his hair. How could he have missed this? ''I haven't gotten any notes from his teachers.''

''Interims came home today,'' Felicity said. ''Jacob's afraid he's going to flunk second grade.'' She paused. ''He's terrified of disappointing you.''

His heart clenched. ''Me?'' He turned around. ''If he's having problems, we just need to find a way to help him. Why would I be disappointed in him?''

The expression on her face gentled. ''He wants to be just like you,'' Felicity said. ''He wants to be an Iggy.''

Huh? ''An Iggy?''

''A graduate of Texas M&—''

''Texas A&M,'' he said, shaking his head. ''Aggie,'' he corrected her, thinking his father would turn over in his grave if he'd been called an Iggy. Lord, what a night. He sighed. ''I'll talk with him tomorrow.''

''Bree brought home her interim report, too. All As.''

''No surprise there,'' Brock said, proud of his daughter and hurting for his son. ''Jacob probably wants to feed her fire ants.''

Felicity nodded. ''It's tough for him.''

Frustration surged through him again. ''Why did you know this when I didn't? These are my kids.''

Felicity shrugged. ''I was just here.''

''Addie was here and she didn't know.''

''It was timing, just timing.''

''I don't want my kids getting attached to you.''

"They won't," Felicity assured him, her voice impatient. "I'm not really good with children."

Brock frowned in confusion. "What makes you say that?"

"Because it's the truth. I never took any child psychology courses. The only experience I have is that I was once a child myself. An imperfect child who didn't quite measure up, with a mother who was very busy with parties and a father who I suspect called me Princess because he couldn't remember my name."

Brock heard the heartfelt ability for empathy in her words, but wanted to deny the power of it. He didn't want Felicity to be good with his kids. He didn't want her interference. He didn't want to think that beneath the flightiness and the weight of her dollar signs, she was a very special woman. He didn't want to, but his innate sense of fairness compelled him. It cost him, though.

"If you want to help Jacob in the afternoons, I'll be obliged," he said, looking at her still-damp clothes and hair. He stopped himself before he warned her not to catch a chill. He clenched his jaw, telling himself she wasn't his concern. "But I don't want him to get too attached to you."

She gave a sad smile. "I don't think you need to worry. I can't remember very many people getting too attached to me. Maybe attached to my money, but not to me."

If she dwelled on her brief discussion with Brock very long, Felicity thought the following afternoon, it could depress her. As she'd pulled off her wet clothes last night, the aloneness closed around her again.

Brock didn't want her here. He didn't want his children growing attached to her, which was a near impossibility as far as Felicity could see. In every way a human being could use a hug, she could have used one last night.

She'd gone without. It wasn't the first time and it certainly wouldn't be the last. After spending much of the day trying, in vain, to discover her occupational future, she'd helped Jacob with his homework. She was certain she'd helped, but wanted to do more, which meant she needed more information, which entailed another trip to the bookstore.

Addie's arthritis was still bothering her and Brock was busy in the north pasture again. That left two options: walk or risk the wrath of Brock by hitching a ride.

Felicity supposed she couldn't get much lower on his totem pole, so she chose direct disobedience. If she was lucky, she would get back before Brock did. Besides, Ray was harmless, she thought as he dropped her off at the bookstore.

An hour later, she walked out of the store with several books, Internet software and a computer catalog.

"Hey, Flip," Ray called, sauntering from the curb. "You've got a bunch of books. Before you bury your pretty little nose in them," he said, brushing his finger over her nose, "you should take a break. Let me buy you a drink at the Longhorn Bar."

Felicity shook her head and glanced at her watch. "I need to get back. I'm sure Brock is expecting you, too."

"No rush. It's almost Friday night. Everybody deserves a little time off," he said, leaning closer.

Felicity felt a prickle of unease. She stepped backward. "I really need to get back."

"Just one drink, Flip. Just one. You won't regret it."

"You're sure I can't persuade you to take me back now?"

"You gotta let me buy you a drink," he said.

"Okay," she said, reluctantly realizing she was stuck. "Just one and then we go back to the ranch."

The Longhorn was just a few blocks away, and the locals had started the weekend early. The bar was already crowded with men and women. The sound of country music bounced against the walls and beer flowed freely.

With no white wine in sight, she sipped sarsaparilla while Ray downed two beers. He'd found a table in a darkened corner, and her eyes were finally adjusting to the lack of light. She glanced at her watch.

"Dance with me," he said.

"Oh, no," she said, disconcerted. "We were just going to have one drink. Remember?"

"C'mon," he said, stroking his fingers down her arm. "Just a little two-step."

"I don't know how," she told him, shifting away from his touch.

"I'll teach you," he said, standing.

"I don't really—"

He urged her to her feet. "C'mon. We can dance back here where no one will notice us."

Felicity felt his arms close around her. "You promised we would leave after one drink," she reminded him.

"Loosen up," he told her, meshing his lower body

with hers. "We could have a good time. I can take care of you."

She pushed against his shoulders. "I want to go back to the ranch."

He slid his fingers through her hair and lowered his mouth. Felicity felt a rush of panic and complete distaste. She turned her head and his mouth landed on her cheek. One of his hands slid up just beneath her breast. "Stop!" she whispered frantically and kicked his shin.

Ray swore. "Wha-what the hell's your problem?" he demanded.

He loosened his hold and Felicity took advantage of the moment to stumble out of his arms. Her heart hammering a mile a minute, she grabbed her bags and wobbled out of the bar.

Disgusted, upset and distraught, she walked away from the bar. Her primary objective was to place as much distance as possible between herself and Ray. When she found herself back in front of the bookstore, she took several deep breaths and tried to decide how she would get back to the ranch. She obviously wasn't going to ride with Ray. There were no taxis, she realized with sinking realization. She would have to call Addie.

Locating a pay phone, she dialed the number. "Addie," she said, relieved when the housekeeper answered.

"Miss Chambeau, I've been worried about you."

"I've had a little…" She paused. "…transportation problem. I apologize for troubling you, but I need a ride—"

"Oh, Mr. Logan's headed into town for you now."

Felicity's stomach sank to her feet. "How did he know where I was?"

Addie chuckled. "Well, there ain't a lot of choices. We figured you'd gone shopping. Where are you?"

"Near the bookstore," Felicity said, dread seeping through her blood.

"You sit tight and I'll call him on the cell phone. He'll be there in no time."

"That's what I'm afraid of," Felicity murmured after she hung up, wishing she'd thought to bring her own cell phone. A jet would be nice right now. A jet to Tahiti. Siberia. Anywhere away from Brock Logan.

Five

―――

"**Y**ou were right. I was wrong. I apologize," Felicity said before Brock could deliver even one of the blistering admonitions that had raced through his mind on his way to collect her.

Although she was overdressed for the little town of Blackstone in her knee-length cream skirt and silk blouse, he noticed her hair was slightly mussed, she was biting her lip and she looked upset. Ignoring his offer of assistance into his truck, she avoided his gaze and climbed in under her own steam. Despite his frustration and her awkwardness, he noticed the mesmerizing way her skirt pulled tight over her hips as she maneuvered. Felicity might be a pain in the rear, but she also had a great rear end.

Brock closed her door and walked to the driver's

side of the truck. "Is Ray at the Longhorn?" he asked after he got in.

She closed her eyes. "Can we please just go back to the ranch now?"

"What did he do?"

She hesitated. "Before or after I kicked him?"

Brock felt his temperature rise. "Did he touch you?"

"He tried," Felicity admitted. "After I went to the bookstore, he wouldn't take me home until I agreed to one drink at the bar. He drank more and wanted to dance in the corner. When I refused, he got—" she faltered "—pushy."

Brock felt the bitter taste of anger rise to his throat. "Is he at the Longhorn?"

"Yes," she said quietly.

Brock drove in silence to the bar. "Stay here," he told her before he headed inside. He collected the keys to the ranch truck from Ray and told the bastard not to return to the Triple L. It took every bit of his restraint not to punch Ray.

Returning to the truck, he started the engine and drove quietly with his hands clenched around the steering wheel for several miles. When he could speak in a normal tone, he said, "I told you to stay away from the men, Felicity."

"I know," she said. "I'm sorry, but I needed to get to the bookstore today."

"Books for what?" he demanded.

"I wanted some books about helping children with reading problems."

Her explanation scored his heart and rained on the fire of his anger like an afternoon shower. He took a deep breath and inhaled the soft, sexy scent of her perfume. How could he chastise her for trying to help his son? And getting mauled for her effort, he thought, his anger at Ray rising again. The image of Ray touching her made his gut twist in a vicious knot.

"Next time ask Addie or me," Brock said, bothered by how much he didn't want another man touching her.

"Addie felt bad and you were busy. I didn't want to bother you. I had decided to extend my stay for a month because of Jacob and because my vocational quest isn't exactly progressing at warp speed, but I'm sure you'd rather I leave," she said. "Would you mind letting me out a few minutes before you turn in the driveway?"

He tossed her a quick glance and frowned. "Why?"

"Because I'm not ready to go back to the guest room. I need to be outside for a few minutes, to walk," she said, her voice unsteady. "To breathe."

He could see she was still tense and upset. Brock took a deep breath of his own and turned in a different direction. "I know where to go." Driving down a dirt road, he pulled to a stop at a fence next to a stream.

"Where are we?"

"We call it High Lonesome. The most peaceful spot on the ranch," he said, getting out of the truck, opening her door and offering his hand to assist her. "Good for what ails you."

She hesitated before she accepted his help, making him prickle in irritation. Her hand felt soft in his and he felt an odd urge to twine his fingers through hers so he could feel her against the insides of his fingers, too. She pulled away, however, leaving him with a restless sensation that lingered.

Ever polite, she murmured, "Thank you."

In the evening dusk, he watched her walk toward the stream. She stopped next to an old tree, and heedless of the rough bark, leaned against it with her arms wrapped around her slim frame. She presented a strange, but pleasing picture dressed in her city clothes, standing in a pasture.

She was a strange, but sometimes pleasing woman, he thought, moving toward her, unable to avoid the fact that she looked very lonely.

"It's beautiful here," she said. "The sound, the peacefulness. I'd like to stay awhile. You can drive to the ranch and I'll walk back."

He glanced at her high heels dubiously. "In those?"

"I'm from New York. I can walk a mile in stilts. You can go back. I'll be here." She glanced at him with a wry smile. "I can't cause too much trouble here."

"You want to be alone," he said, fighting another itchy urge to touch her hair.

"I want to take a little break from disrupting your life," she said.

"It hasn't been all bad."

She glanced at him sideways. "Feeling sorry for me? No need. I'll be fine. I am fine," she insisted as if she were trying to convince herself more than him. She pushed away from the tree and walked closer to the stream. He watched her stumble on a root and pitch forward.

Brock rushed forward to help her.

"I have a little coordination problem," she said

breathlessly. "I told you that you should go," she said, clinging to his arms. "That way, you won't feel compelled to rescue me from myself."

Brock didn't say anything. She felt so good in his arms he was wordless.

"But rescuing is part of your honorable character, isn't it? You've probably always known exactly who you were and what you wanted and how to do it. Do you have any idea," she asked irritably, "how incompetent you make the rest of us feel?"

His lips twitched. "Is that a compliment or insult?"

She ignored his question. "You're strong, *coordinated*," she said in an accusing voice. "You speak and your cowhands obey. You're effective and intelligent. You have two wonderful children and a brother and sister. Is there anything you don't have?"

"A wife." The word sprang unexpectedly from his tongue, deep from his heart. He instantly regretted it.

"She was obviously a flake," Felicity said in a dismissive, matter-of-fact tone. Her assessment was voiced with such confidence that he felt as if she'd tossed one of the weights he carried into that stream. And she'd done it so easily.

He looked into her guileless gaze and a kick of need ricocheted through him all the way down to his boots. It struck Brock that he couldn't remember the last time he'd held a woman in his arms when day was turning to night. The restless sensation in his gut drew tighter. Her breasts brushed against his chest; her torso meshed with his belly. It would be easy to dip his head and touch her parted lips with his, to taste and take her with his tongue. It would be easy to slide his leg between her silky thighs and draw her even closer.

It would be so easy, but she'd just been pawed by another man she hadn't wanted touching her, he remembered, yet still didn't release her. He could touch her hair, he thought. That would be safe. He lifted his hand.

Her gaze shifted as if she sensed a change from him. She stood very still while he fingered her hair. Then she took a shallow breath and swallowed. "Did you know your daughter told me that your sister said you need a woman to drive you crazy on a regular basis?"

Surprised, he stopped mid-stroke. "Crazy?"

Felicity gave a little nod. "I don't think she meant crazy the way I make you, though. I think she meant man-woman crazy. And I don't make you man-woman crazy."

Impatience scored his already heated blood. "Why wouldn't you make me man-woman crazy? I'm a man. You're a woman."

"Yes, but you're too honorable to be attracted to—" She broke off when he shook his head.

Brock ground his teeth. "I may have been raised to do the right thing, but I'm still a man," he told her, thinking he was a man who could want the wrong kind of woman. "You may be impulsive and you may not think the same way I do, and you sure as hell don't do things the same way I do, but you've got a good heart."

Felicity blinked, then her face lifted in a big smile. "Think so?"

"Yeah, but you need to understand that I'd like to see you out of that skirt and blouse and find out what you're wearing underneath," he said, watching her eyes grow wide with surprise. "The only thing holding me back right now is I don't want to be the second man this evening to push himself on you."

She stared at him for a full moment, then her gaze slid away, but she didn't move from his arms. "You're not pushing," she said in a low voice.

He felt the curl of need swell in his belly. "I feel like pushing," he said, and expected her to pull back.

Slowly lifting her ambivalent gaze to his, she still didn't move away. Instead, she moved closer, pressing herself against him, stretching her arms around him, and tucking her head under his chin.

"Your technique is very different from Ray's," she said. "I don't have the overwhelming urge to kick you."

She moved her head from side to side, rubbing her soft hair over his throat. He could imagine how her hair would feel rubbing other places on his body. Insanity, he thought. There were two ways to settle this; leave or kiss her.

Leave.

Instead, he nudged her chin upward with his thumb and kissed her. Back and forth, up and down, he explored her soft lips. Darker needs tugged at him. He plunged his tongue into her mouth and she opened for him, and the air seemed to crackle around them.

He felt her stand up on her toes to slide her fingers through his hair. The gesture arched her body into his. She wiggled as if to get closer. The instinctual, unbearably sensual little movement made him sweat. Brock took full advantage, sliding his hands down to her hips to guide the part of him that ached into the cradle of her thighs.

He sucked her tongue into his mouth, wanting to

devour her, wanting to slide inside her and feel her moistness close around him and pump him into next week.

Felicity pulled her mouth from his and dipped her head. "Oh, wow. I wish you liked me."

Her words broke through the haze of his arousal. Perplexed, Brock stared down at her backside as his body still throbbed from her closeness. The woman confused the hell out of him. "*Liked* you?"

"Yeah," she murmured and sighed. "I can feel—" she said "—that you want me." She slowly lifted her gaze to his, her eyes dark with a passion that revealed she wanted him, too. "But I wish you liked me."

Hell.

Later that night, Brock couldn't sleep. His mind and body wouldn't let him. Unfortunately, a late-night sandwich wasn't going to take care of his persistent gnawing hunger.

He'd mentally listed a dozen reasons why he couldn't take Felicity to bed, including the Logan Curse, but his body wasn't listening. His room, his private haven, suddenly seemed too small. He prowled his father's study instead.

Drinking a beer, he walked around the room and eyed the piano warily. Since his father had died, Brock had felt uncomfortable in the room until he'd found Felicity playing the piano and swearing at the sounds. It had seemed such a sad room, a room full of his father and his father's heavy grief.

Now, it seemed dusty but expectant. He fingered a few of the keys on the piano, muttering his agreement with Felicity's assessment of the terrible tuning.

"I thought I heard a ghost," Tyler said from the door, looking at Brock in amazement. His brother wore his white hospital jacket and weariness around his eyes.

"No ghost. I'm just restless tonight," Brock said, determined to turn the attention away from himself. "How was your day?"

Tyler sighed and loosened his tie. "Okay," he said. "I specialized in pediatric cardiology and there's not much call for it around here. I can't put in ear tubes every day the rest of my life."

Brock heard the restlessness in his brother's voice. He'd heard it more often lately. The local hospital was too small for anything more than general cases, but Brock figured Tyler would get over his impatience. He always did. "Maybe you'll get a little kid with a heart problem tomorrow."

Tyler threw him a sideways glance, then walked into the study. He glanced at the bare windows and uncovered piano. "If you're redecorating, I like it," he said.

"Not me," Brock said, then reluctantly added the most powerful disruption the Triple L had experienced since a tornado had hit a few years ago, "Felicity."

Tyler raised his eyebrows, then chuckled. "Ah. Our resident goddess."

"I hadn't thought of that description for her," Brock added wryly.

"Then you're the only one. I heard a bit of interesting news today. There's been an anonymous six-figure donation to the hospital."

"Felicity," he said again, wondering if she'd developed amnesia about their agreement.

Tyler lifted his hands in defense. "Hey, I can't swear to it," he said, clearly hearing the disapproving tone in Brock's voice. "She's not getting under your skin is she?"

"Like a burr," Brock said, sitting down on the piano bench.

"She's not all bad," Tyler said, joining him on the bench and lazily playing the melody of "Chopsticks."

"I didn't say she was." He picked out the bass. His mom would have said the low keys sounded thuddy.

"Then why do you look like you think the next hurricane should be named after her?" Tyler continued, picking up the tempo.

"Not a bad idea," Brock muttered, still playing. Lord, it had been a long time. His mother had required both him and Tyler to learn. A few sweet memories trickled in. It had been over twenty years since he'd touched a piano. "Felicity's a part-time job when I'm already working overtime."

"Any chance she'll be leaving for New York soon?"

"Not soon. One of her financial advisors left the country with some of her funds."

Tyler whistled and stopped. "Is she broke?"

Brock chuckled. "Nowhere near it, but it doesn't sit right with me and her New York attorneys aren't getting a damn thing done. I called our retired Ranger friend, Steve, and I'm shipping him down to South America for a weekend of stomping out American cockroaches."

"Bet you wish it wasn't calving season and you could go," Tyler said, tinkering with the treble keys.

Brock felt the temptation burn through him, but shook his head. "I've got better things to do."

"Like Felicity?" Tyler said with a sly grin.

"You're forgetting the curse," Brock reminded him, wondering how Tyler could get involved with women and remain unscathed.

"Maybe you should take a vacation from the curse."

Brock remembered his divorce and swallowed a bitter taste. He took a long swig of beer. "I already took a vacation from the curse. I'm still paying for it."

Tyler sighed and stood. "I like what Felicity did to this room. Maybe you ought to let her redo your bedroom, too," he hinted and ambled toward the door. "By the way, your timing's a little rusty, bro. Mom would make you practice."

"Your finger positioning needs work. It always did."

Tyler met his gaze, and Brock remembered their ongoing competition to be the brightest in their mother's eyes. It was the only reason they'd endured the piano lessons. "I'd forgotten how much I missed her," Brock said, breaking the long silence and looking at her portrait on the wall.

"Me, too," Tyler said, glancing at the portrait, then giving Brock a thoughtfully assessing look. "You can enjoy a woman without falling in love with her. You could use a woman in your life."

"Like a hole in the head," Brock replied. The Logan Curse never quite left his mind.

A couple of afternoons later, Brock stepped through the front door and heard sounds from the study. He tensed in automatic response, wondering what she might be doing this time. He walked down the hallway and stood outside watching.

While Jacob played a cassette and mouthed the words of the book he was looking at, Bree perched on the piano bench. Felicity was clutching something that resembled a slender crowbar and it appeared she was destroying the guts of his mother's piano.

"Middle C," Felicity said, "Hit it."

Bree obliged.

Brock cleared his throat, and Bree spun around. "Hi, Daddy! We're tuning the piano!"

"Is that what you're doing?" he asked, unable to keep the doubt from his voice.

"Yep, Felicity got a bunch of stuff in the mail today."

Felicity pulled her head out of the piano and looked at Brock. Her gaze held a fleeting, but powerful sexual punch, that gave him a buzz. "Express mail is wonderful, and I never realized what you could buy and learn through catalog shopping."

"Piano tuning?" Brock asked.

She smiled, and Brock felt the buzz again. "Yes. There's a computer program for it, so I'm getting another skill. Who knows? This could be my occupation."

Brock imagined men calling her to tune their pianos once a week. "Uh, huh. You've been busy."

"I have a goal."

"Felicity says she might teach us how to play the piano," Bree said.

Felicity glanced at him cautiously. "If that's okay with your father," she said. "It's a beautiful instrument, and once we get the sound right, it would be a waste not to use it.''

Jacob ripped off his earphones and left the window seat. "I'm done. Are you gonna show us how to play 'Chopsticks'?"

Brock blinked. Jacob's enthusiasm was usually reserved for food or roping calves.

Jacob caught sight of Brock and his demeanor immediately changed. His son shoved his hands in his pockets. "You can show us," Jacob said, "but I won't play 'cause girls play piano and guys don't. Right, Dad?"

Felicity shot Brock a disapproving glance. "I'm afraid to guess where he may have picked up this macho nonsense.''

Brock chuckled, walking to the piano. It was nice to see Felicity making the wrong assumptions instead of him. He sat down on the bench. "Not from me," he said, and began to play.

Felicity dropped her jaw in astonishment. She shook her head, unable to believe what she was seeing. She watched his big hands play a little, springy minuet by Bach. Those same hands worked the ranch. Those same hands had held her.

The fact that he made music with those calloused hands intrigued her. A college graduate with honors who roped calves and played the piano. A renaissance cowboy?

Addie stepped into the doorway. "Oh, my stars," she said, putting her hand to her throat. "I thought there must've been a ghost."

"Dad's playing the piano!" Jacob said in amazement. "Do you know 'Chopsticks'?" he asked Brock.

Brock nodded. "I think I might remember it. I'll teach it to you after dinner. You two go ahead and wash up."

Jacob and Bree zipped out of the room with Addie, leaving Brock and Felicity alone. She eased beside him on the seat. "Hidden talent?" she asked.

He shrugged. "I might have one or two."

She lifted one of his hands in both of hers. "When did you learn?"

"Before my mother died. She taught Tyler and me. I'm better," he said.

She laughed and couldn't resist asking, "Better at what?"

"Everything except being a medical doctor," he said, his eyes darkening with intense sexuality.

Felicity felt her heart rate pick up. "Everything," she murmured. "That covers a wide spectrum." His hands fascinated her, large enough to hold a football, calloused and tough. She could feel the controlled strength. She brushed her fingertip over his palm and watched it swallow her finger.

He lifted her finger to his lips, touching it with his tongue, and Felicity's breath stopped in her throat. She felt her breasts grow swollen. Those hands, she wondered, Brock's hands. How would he hold her? Touch her? Take her?

Feeling herself sinking into his gaze, into him, she swallowed hard and tried to clear her head. "Brock," she said, her voice husky to her own ears. "I want to learn to drive a truck."

Six

"**A**bsolutely not!" Brock gripped her finger and stared at her as if he was more certain than ever that she had lost her mind.

It wasn't the first time he'd looked at her that way, Felicity thought and forged ahead anyway. "It's a skill, an important skill," she said.

"It's also insanity," Brock said. "Have you forgotten it's calving season?"

"I try," she murmured under her breath, wishing she could help him forget it for a few moments, too. "It can't be that difficult. I may not be coordinated, but I'm reasonably educable and very motivated."

"No," Brock said, standing. "You're going back to New York soon anyway. Why do you need to drive?"

His words stung in several ways. His eagerness for

her to leave hurt, and his uncaring attitude twisted like a knife. "Would you say that to your daughter or sister?"

He paused. "Maybe not, but you're not my daughter or sister."

"Driving is a life skill. Couldn't you see that teaching me to drive would be contributing to my independence?"

Brock shook his head. "It will contribute to my insanity, and trust me, Felicity, I'm fighting to keep it. Pick another guy, another time."

The rest of Brock's week was demanding as hell. Chronically broken fences on the wrong side of his property, cattle with the wrong brand wandering on his land, his cattle wandering onto the Coltranes' land. Brock scowled at the scrapes on his hands and forearm. Dodging cattle hooves and fixing fences in the dark wasn't the most pleasant way to spend a Friday night. All he wanted right now was to clean his scrapes, drink a beer and go to bed.

It was late. The house was dark except for the lamp in the foyer and a light emanating from the kitchen. He heard a soft sound and wondered who was still awake.

Felicity, wearing her long silk robe and with her hair damp from a shower, stepped out of the kitchen carrying a glass of milk and a plate with a small piece of pie. She stopped abruptly when she saw him.

The trace of guilt that crossed her face amused him. Not enough to smile, but it amused him. "Sweet tooth tonight?"

"It's fudge pie," she whispered. "And if there's any left after tomorrow afternoon, I'll be shocked."

"Bree and Jacob love it."

"Jacob would have eaten the entire pie if he'd been allowed," she said, aghast. "Which would have left none for me."

He couldn't resist teasing her. "I didn't have any dinner tonight."

"There's vegetarian chili in the refrigerator."

Brock dipped his head in shock. Surely he hadn't heard correctly. "*Vegetarian* chili? There is no such thing, not in Texas. Not on a cattle ranch for pete's sake."

"Sure there is," she said with a smile so bright he needed his shades. "I got the recipe off the Internet and since you weren't going to join us tonight, Addie helped me make it. It had grated low-fat cheese on top. The kids loved it."

His father wouldn't just turn over in his grave, he would turn over, grab his weapon and start shooting. "Vegetarian chili," he muttered. "Those are fightin' words. Just don't tell any of the hands or the neighbors or we'll never live it down. That pie looks good," he said, licking his lips.

She pulled the plate against her protectively. "There are two teensy slivers in the corner cabinet behind the dried beans."

"But yours is ready-to-eat."

"By me," she said firmly. She gave him a wary once-over and her gaze stopped at his hands. "How did you hurt your hands?"

"Fixing a fence that borders a cranky neighbor."

She paused for a long moment, her face the picture

of indecision, then she sighed. "Okay, come in the kitchen. You can have the pie, and I'll clean your boo-boos."

He twisted his mouth in irony. "It's been a long time since anyone called my scratches boo-boos." It had been a long time since he'd allowed anyone to tend to him. The only reason he allowed it tonight was because he was so tired.

"What about your dad?" she asked, leading the way back to the kitchen. Setting the plate and milk on the table, she reached into a cabinet and collected the first-aid kit and a cloth. She dampened the cloth and walked toward him.

"My dad wasn't much for babying us, especially after my mom died," he said, sitting down in a kitchen chair.

She pulled her chair next to him, sat, and gently cleaned his hands. "That must have been terribly sad for all of you."

"Yeah. I don't think my dad ever recovered. He would have done anything for her, and she made the sun shine for him."

"How long were they married?"

"About twelve years."

"That's more love than some people see in a lifetime," Felicity said, her voice holding a hint of longing.

Brock let his gaze linger on her soft shiny hair and followed the strands down to her chest. The silk robe gaped slightly, revealing the swell of her naked breasts and one of her nipples. His body responded to the sight, to his ongoing need. He glanced away. "I hadn't thought of it like that, but I guess they were lucky in a way. My marriage never came close to theirs.'' He cleared his throat. ''The Logan Curse strikes again,'' he muttered.

She glanced up at him quizzically. ''The Logan Curse?''

He shrugged. ''Yeah. Historically, the Logan men haven't done too well with women. We tend to lose them.''

''You don't really believe that, do you? That you're cursed?''

''I didn't put much stock in it until I got a divorce. Since then, I decided to stay on the safe side.''

''Which is?''

''No more marriage for me,'' he said.

She nodded thoughtfully. ''Oh.''

''No woman is going to hear me say the words 'will you marry me?'''

She nodded again, smoothing antibiotic cream on his scrapes. ''So, does that mean you've totally sworn off women?''

He shook his head slowly, entwining the fingers of one of his hands through hers.

''You should be nicer to your hands,'' Felicity said softly.

''Why?''

''A musician should always protect what he uses to make music.''

Brock chuckled. ''I don't think of myself as much of a musician.''

She gave a secret, sensual smile. ''Your children do.''

He caught a hint of her sweet scent and felt the

brush of her silk sleeve against his wrist. She was too far away. Tugging gently, he drew her onto his lap.

"You haven't eaten the pie," she said in a slightly breathless voice.

"I don't want pie right now," he told her.

She swallowed, her eyes darkening with arousal. "Then what do you want?"

"I want to kiss you," he told her, sliding his thumb under her chin. "I want to find out what's under this robe."

Her breath hitched. "Nothing interesting."

"Nothing interesting or nothing?" he asked.

She didn't speak, but let him lead her lips inexorably closer to his.

"Nothing to say?" he prompted.

"Not aloud," she said and closed the distance between her mouth and his. Her lips were soft and tender, hungry. He felt her hunger in the stroke of her silken tongue over his bottom lip and the restless movements of her body. She wiggled her sweet bottom in his crotch, plucking at his frayed resistance.

When she suckled his tongue into her mouth, he couldn't stand it. He pushed aside the flimsy opening of her robe and touched her bare, warm skin. Cupping the swollen globes of her breasts, he fondled her tight nipples with his thumbs.

She moaned and wiggled again, brushing against the part of him that throbbed for her, teasing him, making him so hard he ached. Brock slid his hands down to her waist, then farther. When he found her hips naked, the knowledge blew the top of his head off.

He eased his fingers between her silky thighs and found her hot and wet. He brushed his thumb over her swollen bead of arousal, and she made a soft, sexual sound of longing. That sound made him want to take her on the kitchen table.

She pulled slightly away, licking the taste of him on her lips, and tugged at his shirt buttons. She pushed aside the denim fabric and they both moaned when her breasts meshed with his chest.

Brock rubbed against her, luxuriating in the sensation of her aroused nipples. He couldn't get enough, couldn't move fast enough. He lowered his mouth to take her nipple into his mouth, and she slid her fingers through his nape, urging him on. He continued to stroke her intimately, loving the feel of her wet, tight femininity and the sound of her pleasure.

She lowered her hands to his thighs. He felt her slight hesitation before she caressed him. One more minute, and Brock was sure he would bust his fly.

The front door swung open, penetrating their undivided attention on each other. Pulling back, Felicity stared at him in frozen silence. "Who?" she finally whispered.

Brock tried to clear his head, but it was apparent his blood had settled in another part of his body, far far away from his brain. He shook his head. "Tyler."

The sound of footsteps coming spurred her into action. Glancing down at her completely exposed body, she gave a little squeak. "Omigod!" She scrambled to her feet, turned to the sink, and tied her robe.

Brock fastened a few buttons on his shirt.

"Hey!" Tyler said, entering the kitchen, coming to a stop. "I thought I was in charge of all the late-night refrigerator raids in this house."

Out of the corner of his eye, Brock saw Felicity

sprinkle water on her face and reach for a glass. "Addie made chocolate pie."

Tyler glanced at Felicity curiously. "And our silent partner has a weakness for chocolate."

She turned and smiled. Brock saw her lips tremble slightly, and vulnerability shone in her eyes. "Always," Felicity said. "It looks like a few of the Logans do, too."

Brock noticed all the telltale signs of their passion, her tousled hair, her swollen lips, the flushed skin of her face and throat, the still-hard nipples thrust against her silk robe. For some odd reason, he didn't like Tyler seeing her this way.

He stood, drawing the attention away from her. "I didn't get any dinner because I was out fixing a fence and collecting my prodigal cattle."

"Uh-oh. Not the Coltranes again."

Brock nodded and took a sip of the milk. At the moment, he would have considered trading his best stud for a bourbon. "It's happened three times during the last six weeks. Some of their cattle end up on Triple L land, and they've accused us of stealing."

"What are you gonna do?"

Brock shrugged. "I can't watch that entire west boundary every minute during calving season, and I can't build a fence through the stream, but I'll send some men to check several times a day. The Coltranes have been a pain in the rear since they set foot in Texas."

"Spoken like a true Logan," Tyler said, then winked at Felicity. "One of the Coltranes developed a fondness for my grandfather's wife and tried to steal her away."

"He didn't just try," Brock corrected, remembering his father's deep-seated bitterness with the Coltrane clan. "He seduced her and she died because the bastard drove off a cliff."

"The theory is that Coltranes are wife-stealers and they think the Logans are still trying to get back at them after all these years," Tyler said. "Then again, if Grandma Logan left Granddad for another man, she must've been unhappy."

Felicity stepped from behind Brock. She appeared to have pulled herself together. "You have a lot of interesting stories in your family history."

"What about the great Chambeaus?" Tyler asked.

She gave a winsome smile. "Maybe a few quirky stories. You have no idea how lucky you are to have siblings and cousins, family," she said. "There are some things money can't buy, and family is one of them." She glanced at Brock, then looked away. "It's my bedtime. Sweet dreams to both of you."

Felicity slowly climbed the stairs and walked past Jacob's and Bree's bedrooms, then past Brock's room to the guest room. She was always careful not to allow herself to call the bedroom where she stayed *her* room because it wasn't. At night, Felicity had time to think. Living with the Logans reminded her of things she would never have, things she craved, like a sense of belonging, being loved. They seemed to have no idea how blessed they were to have all their familial connections.

She wrapped her arms around herself and sank down onto the bed, remembering how Brock had touched her just moments before. She wondered what had gotten into her to make her lose control with him.

She had felt needy and wanton, yet at the same time so needed and wanted. It had been a delicious combination and produced the oddest thrill that she, of all women, could make Brock Logan break some of his iron restraint. Dangerous, she thought.

A knock on the door startled her. "Yes?"

Brock pushed the door the rest of the way open. He carried a plate with a slice of pie. "You missed your late-night treat."

The gesture made her heart tighten, it made her foolishly think she could mean something to him. She blushed when she thought of how he'd touched her and how she'd responded. "Thank you," she said, accepting the plate and turning away from him. She set the cake down on the nightstand. "I—I apologize. I don't know what came over me. I—"

"You're sorry for what?"

She cleared her throat. "My earlier behavior."

"Oh," he said in a voice tinged with irony. "Why are you sorry? Because I told you I would never get married again?"

She whirled around in surprise. "No. Actually that was refreshing."

Confusion and doubt furrowed his brow. "Refreshing?"

She nodded. "Yes, refreshing. Several men have proposed to me. My mother always told me I should never assume that a man who asked me to marry him loved me, or for that matter, wanted me. So, since I know you're not interested in marrying me, then the reason you—" She faltered, but made herself continue. "The reason you kissed me is because well, I affect you."

"Uh-huh," he said, closing the door.

It struck Felicity again that he was so tall, and that the controlled power in the very way he walked just did something to her. If that weren't bad enough the expression in his eyes made her stomach feel as if she were stuck going up the down escalator at Macy's.

"So why are you sorry?"

Felicity felt too warm. "Because I lost control."

"You didn't like it."

"I didn't say that," she said, and wished she hadn't liked it. She sighed. "I know we're not suited. You're so Texan, and I'm so New York, and you're just so…male," she said, knowing it sounded lame.

His lips twitched. "That's bad?"

"No." She closed her eyes for a moment to find her bearings, then opened them. "I'm just not sure an affair with you is a good idea."

"Sounds like you know more about what you don't want than what you do want," Brock said, lifting his finger to her cheek, then sliding it down her cheek to her throat. "Maybe you should spend a little more time thinking about what you want," he said, his voice caressing all her secret places.

His gaze kissed her, consumed her, made love to her, sending apprehension and a wicked temptation that sent her into an emotional tailspin. She wondered how she could stand so still when she felt as if she were going a hundred miles per hour.

She swallowed. "I may do that," she said, unable to look away from him.

"Good," he said, sliding his finger lower beneath her robe, dangerously close to her nipple.

Felicity held her breath, and he circled the tender

swollen bead with his finger. When he pulled away, she bit her tongue to keep from crying out.

He lifted the same finger to his mouth and kissed it. "Sweet dreams, darlin'."

He left her then, alone and so hot she was sure her feet would burn holes in the floor. Rushing to the window, she threw it open and drank in the cool night air. Overwhelmed by her arousal, she shook her head. She wondered what Brock would think and do if he knew that for all her proposals, or perhaps partly because of them, she'd never made love with a man. Would he laugh or be angry?

She perched in the window seat and stared up at the big Texas sky. He'd made an important point, though. If she wasn't going to get married, and the convent was out because she was on fire for a Texas rancher, she did need to make some decisions about how she was going to handle her romantic life. She also needed to decide if she had the nerve to have an affair with Brock.

The following week, Brock spent most of Monday night working with a first-time mama who seemed bent on delivering her calf in a stream. She successfully delivered the calf on dry ground, but took her time doing the job. By Tuesday afternoon, he was beat, so he decided to catch a few winks.

As soon as he walked in the front door, Addie greeted him. "The word is out," she said ominously. "You've received three invitations to bring your guest from New York with you to dinner."

Brock bit back an oath and swiped his hand over his face. "Did you tell them I'm too busy?"

"They all said they would be happy to entertain your guest if you're otherwise occupied." Addie lowered her voice. "They also asked if you and Felicity are romantically involved."

Suspicion settled in his gut. "Who were they?"

"The Fosters, McClanahans and Parkers. All have sons of marriageable age."

"With an eye to adding to the family nest egg," Brock said in disgust. "I knew this would happen. It's exactly what I wanted to avoid. Soon the whole damn county will be pounding on my door trying to get at—"

The sharp screech of brakes drew his attention out the window. He glanced at one of the ranch trucks and noticed his brother in the passenger seat. He lifted his hand to wave, when he saw who sat in the driver seat. His blood pressure flew through the roof. "Felicity," he muttered, and stalked through the door.

The truck lurched forward, then stopped again.

Brock reached the truck and counted to ten. He didn't know who to kill first.

"I'm giving Felicity her first truck-driving lesson," Tyler said with a smile.

Brock noticed Felicity didn't look at him. "I can see that. Did you leave your brains on a gurney at the hospital?" he demanded.

"No. She asked me if I would teach her to drive a truck. Driving is something everybody ought to know how to do, so I couldn't turn her down." He tossed Felicity a flirting smile.

Brock clenched his fists. "I'd like to talk with you for a moment."

"Sure," Tyler said easily. "We'll be finished in—"

"Now," Brock said.

Tyler must have read the tone of his voice accurately, because his brother sighed and looked at Felicity apologetically. "Give me a couple of minutes, but don't take off for Mexico."

Brock ground his teeth. Tyler followed him to the porch. "I don't want you teaching her to drive."

"Why?"

"She's leaving, going back to the city. She doesn't need to learn how to drive. I don't want to encourage her to stay here."

Tyler cocked his head to one side consideringly and scratched his chin. "That's a little cold, even for you, considering what she's done for the kids."

"Ty, we just got three invitations inviting her to dinner. Word about her is out."

"I wonder who blabbed," he said.

"Ray probably did after I fired his sorry self."

Tyler did a double take. "You fired Ray?"

"He took her into town after I told him not to, then he pushed himself on her at the bar."

Tyler gave a low whistle. "She really wants to learn to drive. I could tell her I won't do it, but I'm sure she'll be able to find someone else who will."

Brock's blood boiled. "I knew she was gonna be trouble."

Tyler tossed him a conspiratorial grin. "Maybe you should teach her to drive."

"Are you *sure* you didn't leave your brains on a gurney?"

"Unless you want me to do it. The lady's made a legitimate request."

Brock swore.

Tyler grinned. "A beer sounds good to me right now," he said. "See ya later. The lady's waiting."

Brock swore again.

How had this happened? he wondered as he stalked to the truck and opened the door. How in hell had he gotten himself in this position? He was in the mood to tie a crowbar in a knot, not teach a New Yorker to drive a truck.

He finally looked at Felicity. She was dressed in soft pink; pink jeans and a matching pink silk blouse. Her blond hair hung in a shiny curtain over her shoulders. Except for the wary, but defiant look in her green eyes, she looked like a sweet, pretty lady who wouldn't hurt a fly, let alone drive a Logan to drink. "I told you what I thought about this," he said.

"Yes, and I followed your instructions," she said, lifting her chin.

He wondered how her convoluted brain had come up with that line of thinking. "How?"

"You told me to find another man, another time," she said in a voice far too sexy and smoky for her sweet pink attire. "So that's what I did."

Seven

The subtle scent of her perfume must have drugged his senses during the first part of the lesson because thirty minutes later, Brock had a stiff neck, a sore back and a headache the size of his beloved Lone Star State. He might as well have been riding a bronco. He endured Felicity's jarring ride until she improved in at least one area—steering. She still jerked when she turned, but not as much as she had at the beginning. Or maybe he was just becoming numb.

When she slammed on the brakes one last time in front of the house, Brock breathed a sigh of relief and planned to grab headache medication as soon as he entered the door.

Felicity looked at him with a forlorn expression on her face, as if she were braced for disapproving words from him. "I'm a rotten driver," she said, sounding so defeated that he couldn't bring himself to agree. It would have been like kicking a puppy.

"It's your first time. You didn't have an accident," he pointed out.

"I almost hit the fence a couple of times," she countered glumly.

"But you didn't," he said.

"This was the worst ride you've had in your life," Felicity said.

"I've had worse," he said without batting an eye, and he had—on unbroken horses and broncs. He remembered a memorable ride in the back of a truck filled with manure.

"But I'm the worst new driver you've ever ridden with," she continued.

Brock didn't like seeing her beat up on herself. "I ran into a tree when I was first learning to drive."

Her eyes widened. "You did?"

He nodded. "See, I did worse than you did."

She studied him silently for a long moment, then smiled and leaned closer to him. Her sweet scent swam around his nostrils, and he stared at her lips. She had the sexiest mouth he'd ever seen, mobile, full and pink. He would love to see her mouth caressing his body, lingering, licking. He grew warm.

"You're lying, and I really appreciate it. It makes me think you might like me a little bit," she said, brushing her sweet, sinful mouth against his. "Just a little bit."

She gave him a little taste, but Brock was past the time when a little bit of Felicity was enough. He lifted his hand to her chin and gently kneaded her jaw, urging her to open more to him. He plunged his tongue into her silken mouth and something inside him crackled and burned.

She clung to his shoulders and pulled away, dipping her head. "I don't know what to do with you."

"I can help with that," he murmured, sliding his hand up her rib cage to her breast.

"Your children are walking up the driveway," she told him.

Brock groaned. He couldn't remember when he'd had a more frustrating day. His head and loins throbbing, he swore under his breath and pulled back from her. "You're not a secret anymore. You've received three invitations to dinner at neighboring ranches."

Felicity sighed. "You've got to help me give away my money."

"You still haven't told me your plans after you give it away."

"I'm going to be a piano tuner," she deadpanned.

"Try again," he said.

Bree and Jacob walked up beside the driver's door and Felicity rolled down the window. "Hey, kiddos," Brock said.

"Hi, how are the two best second graders in Texas?"

"Ready to play," Bree said and smiled at Brock. "Hi, Daddy."

"I'm hungry," Jacob said. "What are you doing?"

"Your dad gave me a driving lesson."

Jacob scrutinized the truck. "You didn't wreck it, did you?"

Bree walked around to the passenger window and Brock chuckled as he ruffled her hair.

"No, but your dad thinks I should get a job."

Bree made a face. "If you got a job, then you couldn't paint my fingernails."

"Another skill," Felicity said. "I can be a manicurist."

Brock rolled his eyes.

"Are they looking for people to work at the ice-cream store? That would be a great job," Jacob suggested. "You could probably get free ice cream."

"That's three," she said to Brock. "You already rejected my idea of entering a convent."

He slid his gaze over her curves and shook his head. "I still do." He thought about his Ranger friend's upcoming trip to South America. "I'd like you to open a bank account in town and give me the number."

Felicity wrinkled her brow in confusion. "Why do I—"

"Dad, can we go for a ride this afternoon?" Jacob asked.

"After you do your homework," Brock said, and got out of the truck. He walked around the truck and opened the door for Felicity. "For insurance purposes, I'll take the keys."

"Afraid I'm going to drive your truck into town without the benefit of a driver's license?" she asked.

"Let's just say I'm removing temptation. Addie or I will take you into town soon for you to open your account."

"You didn't say why you wanted me to open an account," she said, uneasiness dimming the sparkle in her green eyes.

Brock didn't want to get her hopes up. "I'll let you know more about that later." He turned to Jacob. "Hey, son, did your teacher send anything to me?"

"A note," Jacob said, pulling it from his backpack. "She said for me to keep doing whatever I've been doing."

"Fun with Phonics," Felicity said, walking with them toward the house.

"Taking turns reading at night," Brock said at the same time.

She looked at him in surprise. "I didn't know you'd been reading with him at night."

"Yeah, I have. What's Fun with Phonics?"

"A cassette program that helps kids learn to read. One of the books I read recommended it."

Brock nodded. "I had a conference with his teacher last week and—"

"You did?" she exclaimed.

Her surprise irritated him. "Yeah, he's my kid. If he's got a problem, I'm gonna help him."

"I thought you were too busy."

"I may not be able to be there when Jacob gets home in the afternoons, but there are other things I can do. I take care of my own," he told her, watching the emotions in her eyes shift like facets of a gem. Curiosity, desire, admiration and a shadow of wariness. The combination teased and taunted, and Brock was finding Felicity caused an ache that plagued him twenty-four hours a day. He was going to have to find a way to stop it.

Felicity could have refused Brock's instruction to open a bank account in town, or she could have developed selective amnesia. She could have decided to trust Brock or not trust him.

Despite her experience regarding men and her

money, she wanted to believe he was different. He'd given her many reasons to believe he was. She wanted to trust him. She did. And she didn't.

She hated her ambivalence, so she fought it. When Addie took Felicity into town, she opened the account, then found herself fiddling with the new account checks and information during the return trip. Stifling a sigh of exasperation, she deliberately folded her hands over her lap and glanced at Addie. "How long have you worked for the Logans?"

"Oh, my," Addie said. "I started back when Tyler was born." She shook her head and smiled in reminiscence. "The house was a very different place back then. Mrs. Logan always loved to give parties. Mr. Logan wasn't that crazy about the parties, but he was crazy enough about her to put up with them."

"What was Brock like as a child?" Felicity asked, curious about him. She'd grown entirely too curious about Brock.

"He was a noisy little hellion."

Felicity shook her head in confusion. "You're joking! I would have though he was a quiet, solemn child."

"No. Before Mrs. Logan died, Brock made enough noise for three kids. After she died, of course, everything changed. So sad," Addie said. "It's still sad."

"And Brock's father?"

Addie sighed. "I think that was the worst thing. Those kids lost both parents when their mom died. Papa Mac grieved himself to death. He hurt so much he couldn't give anything to the kids, and he was hard on Brock, expected a lot of him."

Felicity's heart twisted at the loss Brock must have

felt. "But didn't things change when Brock got married?"

Addie rolled her eyes. "Now that was a disaster if I ever saw one. He met his ex-wife at college and asked her to marry him when she showed up pregnant. She hated ranch life and wasn't maternally inclined, if you know what I mean," she said with a frown. "You know what that man needs?"

"What?" Felicity asked.

"He needs a woman who will love him no matter what. He's the kind of man who can handle everything life throws at him, but he'll live longer and better if he has a woman who loves him."

Felicity felt an odd tingling sensation, a clutch of her heart, and heard something inside her click into place. *He needs a woman who will love him no matter what.* Could she be that woman? The thought made her want to jump out of the moving truck.

Could she be that woman? Felicity shook her head in apprehension. She could not be that woman because she didn't love Brock, he didn't love her, she was never going to get married and neither was he.

Her heart still hammering a mile a minute, she took a couple of deep breaths and told herself she needn't ask herself that question again. The matter was settled. Besides, she wasn't even sure she trusted him. Opening the bank account and giving him access to it was a bit like throwing down the gauntlet. If he liquidated her account, she would know she shouldn't trust him.

Over the next few days while Felicity struggled with her ambivalence, she avoided Brock. Every morning after he left she casually asked Addie his plans, then stayed out of his way. To keep herself busy, she continued to tune the piano and bring the study back to life. She talked and studied with the children after they arrived home. She ate a light dinner before he arrived home and retired to the guest room to pace and fret.

Her emotions and doubts seemed to bounce off the walls like a hundred rubber balls. Felicity wondered how Brock was doing. She wondered if he missed her. "Silly," she whispered. He was probably relieved to have her out from under his feet, she thought. Well, boots, she amended.

Too restless to stand one more minute in the room, she decided to take a bath. On her way down the hall, she heard Brock's deep voice coming from Jacob's room. Slowing outside the door, she heard Brock reading, then Jacob followed in a halting, but determined voice.

Her throat tightened. For the next few moments, she stood there listening to Brock and Jacob. The devotion they shared was clear. She heard a slight edge of weariness in Brock's tone, but still he continued. Pieces of her restraint slipped from her grip.

Unable to resist, she sneaked a peek into the room and drank in the sight of Brock stretched out on the bed with Jacob beside him. Her heart turned over at the sight of the two dark heads bent over the book. She saw the way Brock's hand encircled Jacob's shoulder. Encouragement, love, support. She could feel it even as she stood outside the door.

Living with the Logans had made it abundantly clear that she'd been standing outside her entire life, and she didn't want to spend the rest of her years doing the same. She stared at Brock, and a myriad of emotions slammed through her. She had missed him, missed seeing his face, hearing his voice, missed the forbidden promise of his touch. She felt a shocking intense longing to be more to him than a troublesome silent partner. She wanted to be more to him and to do more for him.

Felicity feared the worst.

She feared she was falling in love with Brock.

At that moment, Brock glanced up at her. His gaze searched hers. She felt his hunger echo inside her. Unable to breathe for a full moment, she jerked her gaze from his and stumbled to the bathtub. "Bath therapy," she muttered to herself. Maybe she could wash her crazy thoughts from her head.

After she returned to the guest room, Felicity tried to go to sleep, but her mind and body refused. Surrendering to her insomnia, she tiptoed downstairs and made her way to the study, closing the door behind her. For all the grief in the room, she felt welcomed there, as if the room had been waiting for someone to revive it.

She turned on a lamp and unnecessarily checked the plants she'd placed on the window sills and desk. For lack of anything else to do, she pulled out her tuning instrument and worked on the treble keys. She focused on treble D, frowning at the split sound it produced. She hit it for the tenth time and felt someone's breath on her hair.

Felicity nearly jumped out of her wits. Spinning around, she instinctively raised her hands in the air.

Brock eyed the tuning instrument warily. "You mind putting that down? I don't wanna be next after what you've done to the piano."

Felicity glanced at the tuning instrument poised in

self-defense and slumped in relief. "You shouldn't have sneaked up on me."

He glanced down at his feet clad only in socks. "No boots."

"No early warning system," she said. His hair was slightly mussed as if he'd raked his fingers through it. His eyes looked restless and hungry. For her. Felicity's stomach dipped. The longing in his eyes echoed inside her.

"Haven't seen much of you lately," he murmured, moving closer to her, holding her with his gaze.

The closer he stood, the harder she found it to breathe. "You're a busy man."

"You haven't been at dinner," he said, tilting his head to one side, considering her. "Why are you avoiding me?"

Her heart stalled, and she felt her cheeks heat. "I'm not," she lied, not well. She could tell he didn't believe her.

"Try again," he said, taking the tuning instrument from her hand and setting it down.

"I—uh—" She swallowed hard over the knot of nerves in her throat. It didn't feel like a normal nervous, more like a sexual nervous. She closed her eyes for a second, then opened them. "I haven't known what to do with you," she finally admitted.

"I told you I could give you some suggestions."

Felicity's heart pounded a mile a minute. She would have to be insane to get any more involved with Brock Logan than she already was. Perhaps, Felicity decided, she *was* a little insane. "Maybe you should give me some of those suggestions," she whispered.

"Give me your mouth," he said.

She barely blinked and his hand cupped her nape while his mouth took hers. Pulling her up on her toes, he kissed her as if she were water and he hadn't drunk in days. His tongue slid possessively over hers, inviting, compelling her response. Beneath his gentleness, she tasted raw need and urgency.

Brock smoothed his hand down over her bottom, urging her into his hard thighs. The contact of his lower body might as well have been gasoline. Felicity clung to his shoulders, undulating against him, feeling his hardness against her.

Giving a low growl, he picked her up and set her on top of the piano, then stepped between her legs. "You make me want to rush," he said in a voice dark with sexual intent. He parted her robe with his finger, sliding it from her neck to her thighs. "But I don't want to miss anything." He nudged the spaghetti strap of her chemise down with that same calloused, determined finger.

Felicity felt the tips of her breasts bud against the silky material. He pushed down the other strap and the chemise whispered to her waist. Her breasts were bare to his gaze.

He lifted his finger to one of her nipples and drew a circle around it. His touch was seductive and light, and she wanted so much more. Her heart hammering, she closed her eyes, resisting the urge to push her breast against his hand.

"Stop holding back," he said.

Felicity opened her eyes in surprise. "What?" she managed.

"You said you wanted suggestions about what to

do with me.'' He dipped his head closer to her breast. ''Don't hold back.''

Felicity curled her toes as he rubbed her nipple with his tongue. ''Oh,'' she moaned. She felt self-conscious and needy.

''Show me what you want.''

Felicity closed her eyes again and arched against him. He took her more fully into his mouth and rolled her other nipple with his finger and thumb. Each stroke of his tongue tugged at her most tender feminine places. Unable to remain still, she squeezed her inner thighs around his legs and the worn denim of his jeans sensually abraded her sensitive skin. With his mouth still on her breast, he skimmed his fingers down her belly to her wet, swollen core.

Felicity gasped.

''So good, so sweet. Touch me,'' Brock told her.

Felicity tried to do his bidding, tugging ineffectually at his shirt. A button popped onto the wooden floor. The tiny noise echoed with her fast breaths.

Brock lifted his head and brushed his mouth across her turgid nipple from side to side. Then he lifted his gaze to hers. She felt as if he was burning her with the heat in his eyes. He unbuttoned his shirt and pressed her hand to his bare chest. His heart thundered against her palm.

''There you go,'' he muttered with a too-sexy tilt of his mouth, ''rushing me again.''

She bit her lip and tried to get her mind and body under control. The intensity of her arousal made her feel incredibly vulnerable. Her mouth was dry, her hands shook with wanting, and she couldn't have joked if her life depended on it.

Felicity was in way over her head. Past wanting, past longing, she was falling in love with a man who was determined never to commit himself to a woman. When she looked in his eyes, though, she couldn't fight the sense of destiny.

Eight

"I—uh—don't have anything," Felicity said, vaguely, referring to contraceptives.

Brock shook his head and nuzzled his cheek against her thigh. "I do."

"You do?" she asked, shuddering when he replaced his cheek with his lips.

"I've been carrying since last week." His gaze, sexually dangerous, met and caught hers. "I knew this was going to happen."

He skimmed his mouth up the inside of her thigh and pressed his lips against her intimately. Shocked, yet unbearably turned on, Felicity tried to pull back, but Brock wouldn't allow her.

"Lean back. Let me taste you," he murmured, spreading her thighs further with his hands and setting her feet on the ivory keys of the piano. The sound of her feet on the keys was oddly sensual as his tongue glanced her femininity. She closed her eyes at the incredible sensation of his velvet tongue at her most sensitive place. He stroked and caressed until she felt consumed. The coil inside her grew tighter with each touch. He played her like the piano, pushing her over the top again and again.

"Stop," she whispered, his caresses taking her past the edge physically and emotionally. "I can't—"

He pulled her onto his lap and she straddled him, helpless and trembling from the aftershocks.

"Let's go to the sofa," he said, and carried her to the long burgundy camelback couch. He set her down, then watching her with a gaze full of fire, he pulled two plastic packets from his pocket, unbuckled his belt and tugged off his jeans and briefs. He was large and aroused, and in the corner of her mind, it occurred to Felicity that she should tell Brock the degree of her inexperience.

When he guided her hand to his hardness, however, every thought left her mind except one—the overwhelming desire to please him. She cupped and stroked his tumescence, feeding on his groans of pleasure. Following her instinct, she kissed him intimately, licking him, taking him into her mouth. The strength of her desire and need amazed her.

He swore and pulled back. "Too much," he muttered, his gaze claiming her body, leaving no doubt of his intention. "Not enough. How do you do it?" He put on the protection and thrust inside her.

Too much, she agreed. Her body stiffened in shock at his thorough invasion. Unable to breathe, she stared at him.

He stilled and studied her intently, and Felicity could tell by his expression that he knew her secret. He sighed. "Oh, hell."

He started to pull away and distress crowded her chest. "No," she said, instinctively folding her legs around him. She took a careful breath and waited for her body to adjust to his.

"I'm hurting you," he said.

"Give me a minute," she said. "You're so big," she added, unable to withhold the realization.

Brock closed his eyes and gave a pained half chuckle. When she moved slightly, he swore and met her gaze. "Why didn't you tell me?"

Felicity swallowed. "I kinda got carried away." She lifted her hands to his chest and stroked the corded muscles. "How does it feel?" she asked.

"How does what feel?" His voice was laced with frustration.

"To be inside me."

Brock swore again. "Too good."

"You said you would give me suggestions. What do I do now?"

He let out a long hiss of breath. "Hold on."

She clung to his shoulders as he began to slowly pump inside her. Each stroke stretched her a little more, until she began to move in rhythm with him. She watched him watch her, and the experience was so intimate, so erotic, she was awed by the power of it. She could feel his want and need in every pore of her body. The connection wasn't purely physical. His gaze demanded everything from her, and Felicity gave it.

His breath quickened with his thrusts. Driving into

her one last time, he jerked and moaned with pleasure. Felicity was struck with the wonder that his release had been as fulfilling for her as her own had been. The sense of fate and destiny infused her blood. Was she meant for this man? Was he meant for her?

Silently calling himself every kind of fool, Brock struggled for even breath and a sane mind. He wasn't going to find it when he was buried in Felicity, he realized, pulling away from her and rising from the couch. His body protesting, he turned away and swore under his breath.

Why hadn't she told him? Was she trying to trick him? No. In the hazy recesses of his mind, he remembered she'd voiced concern about contraception.

He didn't know who he was more angry with, himself or her. Had he been so blinded by his desire to take her that he'd ignored signs?

Hearing a slight rustle from the couch, he glanced at her. Her body was nude and bore pink marks from his possession. He wanted her again, and he despised himself for it. Looking into her uncertain gaze, he felt a strange combination of feelings. Frustration, desire, protectiveness.

He sighed. She'd been a virgin. He'd taken her as if she had had the experience of a well-seasoned lover. He walked the few steps to the piano, grabbed her silk robe and returned to the sofa.

He covered her with the robe and put his arm around her. "I don't know what to say."

"Me either," she said in a low voice.

"I still don't understand why you—" He broke off, shaking his head.

"There was never anyone I trusted and wanted enough to go the next step," she said. "It's different with you."

Brock looked into her gaze and felt a sinking sensation. He saw long-term in her eyes. If he wasn't mistaken, he saw something more than passion, and it scared the hell out of him. "I'm not making any more forever promises, Felicity."

Her green eyes clouded, but she nodded. "I know."

"Then why me?" he demanded.

She covered her eyes with her hand. He saw her fingers tremble and felt his gut twist.

"I'm not sure I can explain it. In your world, you've always known your place. It's always been so clear for you what you would do and who you would be. I haven't felt that way about much except giving away half of my inheritance." She dropped her hand and gave a shaky laugh. "I still haven't figured out exactly what I'm supposed to do with my life unless I follow Jacob's suggestion and work at the ice-cream shop. I have that clear feeling of doing the right thing about giving away my inheritance." She took a deep breath and finally met his gaze. "And I had that same feeling about you."

The profoundness of her gaze rocked his world. Brock began to sweat. "But—"

"It's okay," she said, and bit her lip. "I know it's not the same for you."

Brock felt as if he'd stomped on a rose, slammed a cat's tail in the door and kicked a dog all at once. After he'd walked Felicity to the guest room, he returned to his and paced. He'd assumed she was sophisticated, with more sexual experience than any women he'd ever met, let alone bedded. She'd been so responsive that he'd assumed she knew her way around a man. He'd assumed he could take her and it would be no big deal for her emotionally. He'd assumed he could take her and it would be no big deal for him emotionally.

He felt like an ass.

He tossed back a bourbon and hit the sack. It took another endless sixty minutes before he fell asleep and dreams of Felicity flung him from one end of the spectrum to the other. He dreamed he made love to her in his bed. She was hot and sweet, and he couldn't get enough of her, but she made everything seem okay. Next, she was telling him good-bye as she left for New York, and he watched her leave, feeling empty. He dreamed he heard her play the piano, and it struck him that she had brought the music back into the Logan house. The sound of the old piano filled him with sweet nostalgia and a sense of well-being. He dreamed he fell in love with her, with a love that filled him up and consumed him at the same time. He caught a glimpse of the most incredible happiness he had ever experienced. Then he saw her dead on the ground, her body cold, and his heart stopped. The Logan Curse had struck again.

Brock sat up straight in bed, his heart pounding, his skin slick with sweat. He drew several heaving breaths before he regained his equilibrium.

Felicity. It was all just a dream.

Swearing under his breath, he dropped his head to his hands. Now that he'd taken her and felt her body accept his and seen her eyes make love to him, he wanted her more than ever. He called himself ten kinds of foolish and wondered what in hell he was going to do with her.

Felicity sighed when the doorbell rang for the third time after lunch. Bree and Jacob were off from school and she was giving each of them a piano lesson. They'd mastered "Chopsticks." and she had them halfway through the treble part of "Heart and Soul."

Jacob made a face. "It's probably another dumb guy asking you out for dinner."

Felicity hoped not. She'd already turned down two dinner invitations. She was grateful for the distraction Brock's children provided today. Every time she thought about Brock, she was overwhelmed by a complex mix of emotions. She was terrified she was in love with him and self-conscious about their lovemaking experience.

"I don't think Daddy's gonna like this," Bree said.

"Then maybe we don't need to mention it to him," Felicity said as the two kids followed her to the door.

She withheld a groan when she saw another unidentified male. He was big, too. She wondered if there were any average-sized men in west Texas. "Is he one of your father's hands?" she asked in a low voice.

Jacob shook his head.

She sighed again and opened the door. "Good afternoon?"

"Tell Brock Logan I want to see him now or there's gonna be trouble," the man demanded. His face looked as if it were set in a permanent scowl.

The back of Felicity's neck prickled at his tone. She

straightened, wishing she'd worn her heels. "Mr. Logan is busy working. It's calving sea—"

"I know what season it is, dammit. That's why—"

"Excuse me, sir, but please watch your language in front of the children."

His face turned red with anger, then he narrowed his eyes. "Do you know who I am?"

"Of course not, since you opened the conversation with a threat." She forced a social smile and extended her hand. "Shall we begin again? I'm Felicity Chambeau, a friend of the Logan family."

The man glanced at her hand and dismissed it. "The name's Adam Coltrane. My property shares a boundary with the Logans."

"A neighbor," Felicity said, still trying to raise the civility of the conversation.

"Your word, not mine," he said. "We haven't been friendly with the Logans for a long time. You tell Brock if any more of my cattle show up missing, I won't bother calling the sheriff. I'll take care of matters myself," he said, and walked out the door.

Now that pissed her off. Whatever his flaws, Brock was an honorable man.

"I think I should go spit on him," Jacob said.

"And I'll scratch him," Bree said.

And I'll kick him, Felicity thought. "No. This is the twenty-first century. We use words."

Propping the door open, Felicity called to him as he swaggered down the porch steps. "Surely you're not inferring that Mr. Logan is stealing your cows?"

Coltrane turned around. "I ain't inferring. I'm stating a fact. If he knows what's good for him—"

"Perhaps you should build a fence if you're that concerned about it."

The man cocked his head to one side, looking at her as if she had a loose screw. "Lady, you obviously don't know what you're talking about. You can't build a fence through a stream."

"Oh, I don't know. People build walls and fences all over the places. Take a look at the Great Wall of China."

He wrinkled his brow in confusion. "This ain't China. It's Texas. You tell Brock—"

Felicity flipped her hair impatiently. "I'll *try* to remember to give Mr. Logan your ridiculous message, but I have a question for you. Why would Mr. Logan want your cows? He has a ton of cows. Not only that," she said before he could answer her rhetorical question, "his cows are better than your cows. Good day," she politely added for the children's sake right before she closed the door.

Felicity couldn't remember speaking to anyone like that in her life. Aghast, she wondered if she was becoming Texan? She glanced down the hallway to find Addie walking toward them with flour on her hands. "Who was that?" she asked.

Still rattled, Felicity managed a shrug. "Somebody Coltrane."

Addie grimaced. "Oh, no."

"He said Daddy was stealing his cattle," Bree said.

"He's always saying that," Addie told her. "Don't pay any attention to him."

"I still think I should have spit on him," said Jacob.

"He needs a good scratch," Bree insisted.

"He was very unpleasant," Felicity agreed, resenting how the fragile serenity of the past hour had been shattered. "This calls for something loud on the piano," she said. "Then chocolate therapy."

"All right!" Jacob said.

Brock was late for dinner and as hungry as he'd ever been. He was looking forward to a filling meal. The calves were starting to drop more frequently now, which kept him and his hands busy bringing the moms and calves to a separate fenced pasture. He'd been distracted by thoughts of Felicity, and he was ambivalent about seeing her this evening. He didn't want to see her, and he did.

He got his wish. The first one, anyway. After Brock washed up, he walked into the dining room and immediately noticed that although Tyler and the kids were already eating, there was no plate set at Felicity's place at the table. His gut gave a little twist.

"Hi, Daddy," Bree said, giving him a little ray of sunshine.

"Hi, sweet thing. Were you and Jacob lazy bums on your day off?" he asked, teasing her.

"No," Jacob said, focused on a piece of cherry pie. "We played piano with Felicity, ate chocolate and chased off men."

"Chased off men?" he echoed, nodding his thanks at Addie as she put a plate of pot roast and potatoes in front of him. His mouth watered from the juicy aroma. He was so hungry he might go for seconds tonight.

"Felicity is gone," Addie said.

Brock's stomach took a deep dip. Had she already left? "Gone?"

"Yes. I think the Parkers wore her down. She accepted an invitation to dinner at their house tonight. Ron Smith and Seth Liddy stopped by, too."

Brock felt a surge of irritation. He frowned. "Did Jay pick her up?"

Tyler nodded. "In his new Suburban, new Stetson and boots so shiny I needed sunglasses to look at them. I told him to make sure she was home by eleven."

"Tyler says Felicity is our babe-in-residence," Jacob said.

"We have two babes-in-residence," Tyler corrected. "Felicity and Bree."

Bree smiled at her uncle and batted her eyelashes. "Felicity says you're a flirt."

Felicity. Felicity. Felicity. If he heard her name another time, he was going to get sick.

"Not me," Tyler protested to Bree, then turned to Brock. "Speaking of Felicity going places. That was a good idea you had for her to drive one of the older ranch trucks around the driveway. She's getting better all the time."

Brock felt his jaw give an involuntary twitch and set down his fork. He could feel his blood pressure rise. "She's been driving one of the ranch trucks in the driveway?" he asked in a deliberately quiet voice.

Tyler immediately identified the tone and shot Brock a wary glance. "I thought it was your idea."

"No," Brock said, and glanced up at Addie's guilt-stricken face. "You didn't…?"

"She asked and asked, and you haven't had time to give her another lesson," Addie said.

"She could wreck the truck."

"Well, she gave me a check to hold for a new truck in case she wrecked this one."

His head began to pound. "And what if she got hurt?"

Addie winced. "I made her promise to go very slowly. She got the driver's manual and has been studying for the test. She's very determined and I didn't feel right stopping her." She lifted her chin. "Every woman should know how to drive, especially in Texas."

Brock swallowed an oath and pinched the bridge of his nose. The woman was causing an insurrection.

"Daddy," Bree said, "you look like you could use some chocolate therapy."

Jacob nodded. "Yeah. That's what Felicity gave us after she told Mr. Coltrane to build a fence like the Great Wall of China and that our cows are better than his cows!"

"She faced down Coltrane?" Tyler let out a guffaw. "I would've loved to see that. Our cows are better than his cows."

"Coltrane," Brock muttered. He was beginning to think Felicity's effects were spreading like a bad flu.

That evening, Brock sat in the den after everyone had gone to bed. Around ten-thirty, Felicity quietly slipped in the door and began to tiptoe up the stairs. Brock put the cattle-ranching journal aside and strolled to the stairway.

"You've had a busy day," he said.

She stopped mid-step and stiffened. Her body oozing reluctance, she turned around. "Yes, I have. How are you?" she asked politely.

He couldn't see the expression in her eyes because of the dim light, but the black dress she wore couldn't hide her curves. Brock knew exactly how the body beneath that dress felt against his. He took a breath. "Besides learning about chocolate therapy and building fences the length of the Great Wall of China, and checking out the transmission and brakes on the truck you've been driving without my permission, it's been a quiet evening."

Felicity cocked her head to one side. "I'll be happy to buy the truck from you."

Brock felt a surge of irritation. Or heartburn. "I'm sure you would, but I'd just as soon you not break your neck on Logan land."

"If you think about it, your risk of liability is pretty low. It's not as if you would get sued. Remember, I don't have family."

The loneliness she tried to conceal tugged at him. He joined her on the steps. "There are people who care about you."

She shrugged, her eyes shadowed. "Maybe."

"Bree, Jacob, Addie," he said, then paused. In the face of her loneliness, he couldn't deny the truth. He tucked his thumb under her soft chin, wanting her to meet his gaze. "And me."

Nine

And me.

Felicity looked into Brock's blue eyes and felt her heart jump into her throat. Calm down, she told herself. Brock cared about lots of people.

"I care about you more than I should," he muttered in a tough and tender voice that felt like a sensuous stroke on her inner thighs.

He lowered his mouth to hers. Felicity parted her lips, his tongue slipped inside, and her meltdown began. The overwhelming wanting he generated invaded her entire system like oxygen. Her mind was filled with the images of making love with him, of touching him and him touching her.

Clinging to a sliver of good sense, she pulled back. "I would never have thought you would be a tease," she chided him.

He looked at her sideways. "A tease?"

"Yes, a tease. You don't want me, so why are you—"

"I *never* said I didn't want you."

"You were turned off by my inexperience," she insisted.

"I was not. I—" He caught himself as he raised his voice. "Hell!" he muttered with force. Then he picked her up and carried her up the stairs.

"What are you doing?" she demanded.

"Just shut up until I close my door," he said, carrying her into his bedroom, nudging the door closed, and dropping her on his bed.

Felicity landed with a bounce, taking in the masculine comfort of his domain. An oak dresser and bureau lined walls which displayed rodeo belt buckles, an Indian breastplate, and pictures of Jacob and Bree. The large oak sleigh bed was covered with a patchwork quilt in shades of blue and cream. The room, like the man, echoed with a sense of family, refuge and unrelenting masculinity at its best.

She would never share this room with him, Felicity warned her heart. Never.

"I never said I didn't want you, and I was not turned off by your inexperience," he told her. "Surprised, shocked, but not turned off."

"Yes, you were," she said, lifting her hand when he opened his mouth. "You didn't see your facial expression. You looked close to horrified."

"I did not!" He took a deep breath as if he were fighting for control. "I didn't want you thinking we were going to get married."

Felicity felt a tinge of irritation. "I thought I told you I didn't plan to get married."

Brock crossed his arms over his chest and tossed her a skeptical glance. "My experience is that women tend to change their minds."

"Yes, well, you may have a lot of experience with other women, but you don't have a lot of experience with me."

"Are you telling me you haven't secretly dreamed of a big church wedding with a white dress and a reception with dancing?"

"You have to consider my point of reference," she told him. "My parents didn't have a terrific marriage, and my mother took every opportunity to warn me against all the men who would want me only because of the Chambeau wealth."

"And being with me didn't change your mind at all," Brock said, his tone peppered with doubt.

Her pride stung and her heart hurt. How arrogant, she thought, and unflattering. If there were a smidgeon of truth to it, she would never tell him, Felicity thought.

"Exactly," she said. "Just as being with me hasn't altered your opinion. Oh, for heaven's sake!" she said, rising to her feet. "If I'd wanted to get married, Jay probably would oblige, but I'm not—"

"—Jay Parker?" Brock interjected with a frown. "What did Jay do?"

She waved her hand in a dismissing gesture. "Nothing except tell me I was the kind of woman that made him think about settling down. The point is—"

"That snake. That low-down dirty snake. I turn my

head for one minute and—'' He broke off and swore. ''Did he try anything with you?''

''Why would you care?'' she yelled. ''You said you don't want anything permanent with me!''

His eyes glinted with anger. ''While you are at my house, it's my responsibility to keep you safe and to keep my neighbors from preying on you.'' He lifted his finger. ''You haven't made it easy by cruising around in my truck, hitching rides into town, and accepting dinner invitations from folks you don't know.''

Felicity could feel their argument escalating out of control, but she was too offended and upset to stop it. ''If I'm that much trouble, then why don't you tell me to leave?''

Complete silence stretched between them.

''Isn't that what you want?'' she asked, wanting him to deny it. ''For me to leave?''

''Since you're a silent partner—''

''That's bull,'' she said, borrowing the term from Bree and Jacob.

He rubbed his jaw and shrugged his shoulders. ''The kids—''

''Don't drag them into this,'' Felicity said. ''This is about you and me. Do you want me to leave?'' she asked and held her breath.

Brock sighed. ''I won't tell you to leave, but I can't ask you to stay.''

That hurt. She'd wanted just a little encouragement from him, but he couldn't or wouldn't give it. Felicity supposed that was what she got for pushing. She bit her lip. ''Good night, Brock,'' she said and headed for the door.

He reached out to clasp his hand around her wrist. "You're upset."

"Don't worry about it." She shook her wrist free. "I'm not your responsibility."

"I don't want you upset."

"You'll get over it," she said and reached for the doorknob.

Brock put his hand to the door. "Felicity," he said in a voice that made her heart ache.

Her emotions ripping at her, she stared at the oak floor. She couldn't meet his gaze. "Is it so hard for you to say you like me being here?"

She heard him whisper a terse oath, then he took her by her arms and pushed her back against the door. "There's plenty to like about you. I wouldn't be a man if I didn't want you, and it doesn't have a damn thing to do with your money. But let's not fool ourselves, we both know you're leaving. It's just a question of when."

Felicity's heart squeezed tight. She saw something in his eyes, a wanting, that gave her an inkling that perhaps he cared more than he showed. It made her bold. "If you could have me any way for any amount of time, how would you want me?" she asked, and immediately put her finger to his mouth. "Don't answer. I just want you to think about it."

Felicity's question buzzed around Brock's mind like a fly the rest of the evening and the following day. It was a stupid question, he told himself for the tenth time as he met her for another driving lesson. Stupid because it didn't matter what he wanted. He and Felicity couldn't be worse suited for each other, and there was always the Logan Curse.

He had more important things to think about than Felicity's question this morning, though, and so did she, but he would save that news for later. He figured he *and* Felicity needed to keep their concentration solely focused on her driving if they were going to get out of this experience alive.

She dangled the keys to the old truck as she walked down the front porch steps. "Ready?"

He stifled a sigh. "As I'll ever be."

She smiled and gave a chiding shake of her head. "You're going to be surprised. You won't need a neck brace after this ride."

"Traction?" he asked, unable to resist teasing her.

She tossed him a level gaze that was sexy in a wholly feminine way. "Antacids. Prepare to eat your words, cowboy."

They got into the car and Brock watched Felicity fasten her seat belt and adjust the mirrors. She put the key in the ignition and smoothly accelerated. She didn't chat with him, just focused on driving. When she had successfully completed two trips down the drive, Brock was impressed.

"Turn right out of the driveway," he said.

Felicity swung her head to look at him in amazement. "A *real* road?"

He chuckled. "Yeah, a real road."

"Omigod," she said, taking a quick breath. "I can do this," she said more to herself than him. She tossed him a quick glance. "Don't say anything unless it's absolutely necessary."

Brock frowned in confusion. "Why?"

"Because," she said, carefully turning onto the real road.

"Why because?"

"Because I'm pretending you're Tyler. Now be quiet."

Brock didn't like her answer one damn bit. *Tyler!* Why the hell would she pretend he was Tyler! He knew his younger brother appealed to the ladies. Brock had always been the back breaking hard worker. While Tyler worked hard, too, he also played hard and was something of a charmer. Slipping in and out of relationships with women was easy for him.

Sliding a glance over at Felicity as she hunched over the steering wheel with a white-knuckled grip, he wondered if her affections had changed with the wind and she was interested in his brother. He wondered if his brother had gotten caught in her spell.

A bitter taste filled his mouth. He didn't like either possibility. Although Tyler was plenty experienced with women, Brock knew Felicity would have the poor guy in knots in no time.

At the next intersection, he said, "Take a left and turn around."

She gave a small jerk, then murmured something encouraging to herself and straightened. Brock directed her to a quiet area and instructed her to pull onto the dirt road. He was going to straighten Felicity out. He couldn't allow her to disrupt anything else on the ranch, including his brother.

She pulled to a stop and leaned back against her seat, then glanced at him and sighed. Her smile held a hint of triumph and pride. "No whiplash. No traction. When you eat your words would you like sugar and a cherry on top?''

The way she rubbed it in would have usually amused him, but Brock didn't feel like smiling. He cracked his knuckles. ''Why did you want to pretend I was Tyler?''

Felicity's smile faded and she glanced away as color bloomed in her cheeks. ''He's different than you.''

''You didn't answer my question,'' he said, unable to keep a thread of impatience from his voice.

She sighed, smoothing a long strand of hair from her face. ''Tyler doesn't make me nervous,'' she muttered, avoiding his gaze.

It took a moment to register her comment and its ramifications. Brock felt an easing inside him and more than a trace of foolishness. ''I make you nervous,'' he concluded.

''Yes.''

''Why?''

She glanced at him sideways. ''I don't think your ego needs any more feeding.''

His lips twitched in amusement. This was almost worth the agony he'd gone through during the last twenty minutes. ''Why?'' he persisted.

She gave an exaggerated sigh. ''It's obvious, isn't it? I want to impress you. You have no idea how intimidating it is to be around someone with so many practical skills when I have nearly none. Being around you makes me want to learn to do some of the things I've always paid others to do.''

''Like tune the piano and drive a car,'' Brock said.

Felicity nodded.

''Make your bed,'' Brock teased.

Felicity gave him another sideways glance. "You're pushing it. Tell me, Brock," she said, smiling and switching gears, "what does being around me make you want to do?"

"Besides tear out my hair?" he asked.

Felicity shook her head and pressed the door handle. Brock reached across the seat to stop her. "Hold on. Being around you makes me want to lock you in my bedroom," he said, pulling her onto his lap, "and make love to you until neither of us can take any more."

Her eyes turned sultry. "How long do you think that would be?"

Feeling the beginning buzz of arousal, Brock slid his hands over her silk shirt, up her rib cage, just beneath her breasts. He constantly fought the urge to possess her, but sometimes his needs overrode his good sense. He was starting to wonder how best to get her out of his system. Maybe that meant filling himself up with her. Maybe then, he wouldn't feel this insatiable desperate need to feel her and taste her and be inside her.

"A long time," he finally told her, taking her mouth and lifting his thumbs to her nipples.

He swallowed her sigh as he kissed her. The way she melted into him alternately soothed and aroused him. She was so responsive Brock would bet he could take her in the car, pulling her onto his lap and sliding inside her, pumping… Insanity, he thought, pulling back. The woman was a walking invitation to insanity. They would never be right for each other, he reminded himself. Never.

He took a breath to clear his mind, but her perfume

taunted him. It was time, he thought. She needed to know. "Have you checked your bank account lately?"

She shook her head in confusion, her eyes slightly dazed. "No. Should I?" She wrinkled her brow, then looked at him warily. "Is it empty?"

Her doubtful expression was like a jab in his ribs. "Do you really think I would take your money?"

Her eyes widened, and she took a quick breath. "Of course not," she said, but he caught the sliver of ambivalence in her eyes and cursed her cockroach financial advisor and every other man who had been after her money.

"I sent a friend down to South America to do some cockroach-stomping. He happened to run into your former financial advisor and persuaded him to return your money by wiring it to your account."

Felicity threw her arms around his neck. "Thank you, thank you. This is wonderful! Wonderful." She squeezed him, then went very still. "And terrible."

"Terrible?" Lord, this woman was kooky.

Felicity nodded glumly. "I've got to get rid of it soon or I'll end up on that stupid list."

"What list?"

"The wealthiest-women-in-America list. And they always list marital status, which means I'll get more proposals. And the money will just sit there adding up, not doing a darn bit of good."

"Then maybe it's time for you to set up your foundation," Brock said.

"You'll help me?" she asked hopefully.

"I don't know the laws and tax requirements, but I can find somebody for you who does," Brock told her, hoping this wasn't the first slide into a long wacky entanglement with Felicity. He would refer her, then wipe his hands of the matter.

Her eyes grew shiny with unshed tears. She leaned forward and kissed him. "I can't tell you how much this means to me. Now, will you let me buy this truck from you, so I can use it to get my driver's license?"

Brock's stomach twisted. *Felicity on the open road?* "You need more practice," he said, wondering why he felt he needed to protect this woman from herself. It wasn't love, he promised himself. He would never fall in love again.

After they returned home, Brock headed out to the north pasture. When he walked through the door that evening, she practically mowed him down.

"I'm leaving for New York in the morning. I'm already packed," she said, bouncing on her toes. "Your friend did more than get my money back. He brought back Douglas. My attorneys called and they need me to go to New York to make a deposition. While I'm there, I'll be talking with my financial advisors about my plans." She squeezed his arm. "I'm so excited I can barely stand it. I can't thank you enough."

His mind was stuck on her first statement. *I'm leaving for New York in the morning.* He felt as if a bull had kicked him. Brock immediately scolded himself. He should be happy to get Felicity out of his hair for a few days. He could concentrate on the ranch. Hell, maybe he'd get lucky and she would decide to stay. After all, her reason for visiting Texas would be gone. His gut twisted at the thought, but he ruthlessly squelched the sensation.

"Brock, aren't you listening?" she asked, wearing

a huge smile. "Everything's working out because of *you!*" She threw her arms around him. "I don't know how to thank you," she said, then gazed at him for a long moment. "Maybe you can give me a few suggestions?"

She would give him herself again. He could see it in her eyes. His body immediately responded. Why, he wondered, impatient with himself, did this flighty feather of a woman affect him this way?

"You're not saying anything. I'm trying to thank you," she said.

Savoring the softness of her clinging to him, he snatched at the sensations, her scent, the way her breasts grazed his chest and her thighs rubbed his. The sparkle in her eyes usually made him feel lighter, but not now. This could be the last time he held her, he thought, and something inside him rebelled at the prospect. Before Felicity had burst into his home, he'd grown accustomed to living without soft touches and feminine smiles. Before Felicity had blown in from the north like a bad storm, he'd been fine. He would be fine again, he told himself.

Surprised and unsettled by the force of his emotions, Brock backed away and mentally wished her goodbye. "You're welcome, Felicity. Good luck."

Ten

Felicity was sitting on his bed when Brock got out of the shower. She wore her silk robe with not much under it, he suspected, and a feminine smile as subtle as an air raid siren. His heart gave a kick.

Brock frowned at his immediate visceral response. "Problem?"

She cocked her head to one side as if she were trying to read him. "I guess that depends on your point of view," she said. "I've locked your door."

"And?" he asked, towel-drying his hair while he told his blood to stop rushing to his crotch.

"And that could either make you wildly excited," she said. "Or scare you."

"Scare me," he echoed.

"Yes," she said rising to her feet and walking toward him with a Texas-sized dare in her eyes that brought out every primitive instinct he possessed. "Maybe the idea of being locked in a room alone with me might scare you."

No more chipping away at his restraint. She might as well blow a cannonball through it. "You're the one who's not all that experienced. Maybe having sex with me scares you," he said, emphasizing the word *sex* because she was so damn provocative. Her sensual shyness seemed a distant memory.

A trace of uncertainty flickered across her face, but it was quickly gone. "It's more than sex between us."

"How can you be sure?"

She lifted her chin. "If you were going to just have sex with a woman, it wouldn't be me."

"Why?"

"Because you tell yourself I'm a pain in your very nice rear end," she said. "But you actually like me. You might even more than like me, but the very idea of more than liking me makes you incredibly nervous." She gave a slight smile. "Doesn't it?"

Everything about her was making him sweat, but he would be tarred and feathered before he would confess it.

"It's okay, Brock. The idea that little me could make big, strong you nervous is very sexy."

Brock's meager self-restraint ripped. He could almost hear the sound of it roaring through his ears. He dropped the towel from his waist and backed her against the wall. "Is this what you call nervous?" he whispered, pulling off her robe with one swift tug. "Are you teasing me, Felicity?"

Her eyes were round as saucers. For a moment, she stared at him uncertainly. Then she took a breath and lifted up on her toes to stretch her arms around his neck. "I don't want to waste time," she said, and took his mouth.

Brock didn't know it was possible for a man to melt and harden at the same time. He supposed it had to do with different body parts, and Felicity's effect on them. Her bold kiss made him want to lift her up and thrust inside her right now. The tender way she held him made him want to linger. The two needs warred inside him while she slid her mouth over his and arched her breasts against him.

Brock groaned and skimmed his hands down to cup her bottom. Her skin was like silk. Every brush of her breasts against his chest was a delicious, unbearable tease. He lifted her slightly and rubbed his masculinity in the damp notch of her thighs.

She moaned and undulated against him, sucking his tongue deeper into her mouth. She kissed him as if she couldn't get enough of him, as if he were the most important thing in her universe. The room turned into an inferno of his need and her passion. He could see nothing but her, feel nothing but her.

She slid her thigh up the outside of his as if to get closer, and Brock shuddered. He broke away from her mouth. "I want to take you now," he said, taking shallow breaths.

Felicity rippled her pelvis against him in a movement designed to send him over the edge. She was so wet, so hot, and so close to the part of him that ached for her. Closer, she strained against him.

Brock lost it. Everything about her said *take me*. So, he did, lifting her against the wall and thrusting inside her.

She gasped and went still, her hands clinging to his shoulders.

For a terrible second, he was afraid he'd hurt her. "Breathe."

She did, closing her eyes and sinking onto him more fully. "Oh, Brock," she said and gave a low murmur of pleasure.

She felt so good he didn't think he could stand it. "You feel like velvet," he said, drowning in the sensation of how tight, wet and soft she was.

He pumped inside her, and she fastened her legs around his waist. Her breasts swayed temptingly in front of his face. She rolled her hips in delicious counterpart to his thrusts. The tension in his loins roared through his blood until his scalding release tossed him over the top. He felt as if he were falling off a cliff.

Several breaths later, his head began to clear and Brock swore under his breath at what he'd done. He swung Felicity over to his bed, then sat on the side with his head in his hands.

"What's wrong?" she asked. "Did I hurt you?"

Brock's heart swelled at her sincere tone coupled with her ridiculous words. He gave a half chuckle despite the seriousness of his slip. "No, but I didn't protect you."

He finally looked at her. She lay sprawled on his bed naked with tousled hair and witchy sparkling eyes looking like a plunderer's prize. She shook her head and lifted her hand to his cheek. "I used something."

Surprised, he raised his eyebrows. "When did you—"

"I ordered off the Internet. I let my fingers do the walking and overnight mail took care of the rest."

"You ordered contraception off the Internet?"

"Yes. I couldn't think of a good secondary reason for Addie to take me to town," she told him.

Brock sat back against the pillows and pulled her against him. "How did you know we were going to be together again?"

"I just did," she said simply, looking at him with a gaze that held flickers of yesterday and tomorrow.

She looked good in his bed and felt good in his arms. For a moment he wondered what it would be like to have her in his bed and arms more often. Brock immediately shut off the dangerous thought. He opened his mouth to remind her that he wasn't a forever man, then closed it when he remembered she was leaving tomorrow.

"I appreciate all you've done for the kids," he told her.

She stroked his chest. "Your kids are a pleasure, but you know that."

"Pleasure, but not perfection."

"That's okay," she said and glanced at him curiously. "And have I done anything for you?"

"Sure," Brock said. "You've shaved at least two years off my life driving my truck. And my daddy's study will never be the same. You've introduced vegetarian chili onto my cattle ranch and probably escalated my ongoing arguments with the Coltranes and—"

She covered his mouth with her hand. "Enough. I want to know if I've done anything for you here," she said, sliding her hand down to where his heart beat in his chest.

His heart beat faster. "You affect several parts of my body."

Felicity's gaze dimmed. "Parts, huh? I must be greedy. I don't want to affect just parts. I want to affect the whole man."

He tried not to see the longing in her eyes or hear it in her voice. "It's been good being with you. Fun," he said, the superficial term almost making him wince.

Felicity blinked. "Fun? You call what we're doing *fun*."

"You're a fast learner, Felicity."

She stared at him for a long moment, then shook her head and rose from the bed. "You're an idiot."

Surprised by her blunt accusation, he followed her to his feet. "What do you mean?"

Felicity picked up her robe and pushed her arms through the sleeves. "There is something special between us. The way we made love with each other is special."

"You're not experienced," Brock began, reaching for her. "That's why—"

She pulled back and lifted her hands to ward him off. She was hurt and adamant. "It is not. I may not be experienced, but I know the way we've made love is more than fun. And if you really believe that what we're doing here is just fun, then you are an idiot."

Brock sighed. "There's no sense in you getting all upset," he told her. "Especially when you're leaving tomorrow."

Felicity's brow furrowed in confusion. "What does that have to do with this?"

Brock brutally laid out the facts. "Your reason for being here is gone. You can go back to New York and chauffeurs, maids, Macy's and vegetarian meals. You don't ever have to come back here again.''

Felicity's face turned white, and she stood completely silent for a moment that felt interminable. She drew herself up straight and set her chin. ''You're right. I don't.''

She walked out of his bedroom door, and Brock was left with the too-quiet stillness of the room. He should have felt relieved, but her scent lingered; he could still feel her fire, and the taste of her on his tongue. He could still see the expression in her eyes that called to him. He could never answer her call, he told himself. It wasn't meant to be. He would snuff out her memory and the emptiness inside him would disappear, just like Felicity would.

Three days later, Brock struggled with an odd edgy sensation that grew in intensity throughout the day. It gnawed at him just enough to make his temper short. As he watched the kids squabble at dinner, he wondered if a bug was going around.

''You think you're the smartest second grader in the world,'' Jacob accused Bree.

Bree lifted her nose. ''Maybe I am.''

''You can't ride as good as I can.''

''I can read faster.''

''That's enough,'' Brock said. ''You two are individuals with individual talents. Neither one of you is better than the other.''

''Jacob got a D on a book report,'' Bree announced. ''That's why he's in such a bad mood.''

''Blabbermouth,'' Jacob said with a scowl.

''Son, if you needed help, you should have asked.''

Jacob took a bite of pie, then set his fork down. "Felicity was helping me before she left."

Brock's stomach sank, but he pushed the sensation away. "I can help you."

"You're too busy," he said. "Can I be excused?"

Brock stifled a sigh. He *had* been too busy. He'd been keeping himself busy to escape his edginess. He'd made a big mistake by skipping reading with Jacob the last few nights. "We'll talk about this later," he said. "Go take a shower and get out our book."

"Okay," Jacob said and stood. "When's Felicity coming back?"

Brock didn't want to hurt his children, and at this moment, he wished he and his kids had never spent one second in Felicity's presence. "She may not be coming back."

Bree gasped. "She has to come back. She promised she would teach me more piano, and I told her I would teach her how to speak Texan."

"She promised she would teach me piano, too," Jacob said. "And I told her I would show her how to rope a calf." He paused. "She wasn't as interested in learning to brand, dehorn and castrate."

Brock almost chuckled at the thought. Almost. But he saw the concern on his children's faces. They were counting on Felicity to return, and she very well might not. She had no reason to return, he knew, his stomach giving a vicious twist. "You need to remember that her home is in New York."

Bree stood. "It is not. That's just where she was born. She'd rather live here. We want her here. We like her even if you don't!'' On the verge of tears, she bolted for the doorway to collide with Tyler.

"Hey, sweet thing, what's the rush?" Tyler asked with a grin.

"Daddy says Felicity's not coming back, but he's wrong," she said, and ran down the hall.

Jacob quietly followed her out of the room. Tyler reached down to ruffle the boy's hair as he passed by. "Hey, bud," he said, then glanced at Brock with a raised eyebrow. "Looks like everyone's missing Felicity."

"The kids are just a little edgy," Brock said. "A few more days and they'll get used to her being gone."

"Think so?" Addie brought Tyler a bowl of beef stew and he nodded his thanks.

"I know so," Brock said. "Kids have short memories. They get distracted easily."

"Unless they get attached."

"They didn't get attached."

"Right," Tyler said with heavy sarcasm. "That's why Bree is hysterical and Jacob looks like someone swiped his favorite rope."

"Okay, maybe they got a little attached to her," Brock conceded. "But it's not a terminal condition. I'll spend some more time with them and they'll be okay."

"I don't know, Brock. You don't look too good yourself."

Tyler's insinuation that he, too, had become attached to Felicity rubbed Brock the wrong way. "Now what the hell do you mean by that? You know that I know better than to fall for a flighty woman from Manhattan.''

Tyler thoughtfully chewed a bite of stew. "You're probably right. She was pretty and had a body that could stop a clock, but she wasn't the kind of woman that could get under your skin.''

Brock felt a sliver of unease, but he agreed. "Right.''

"I mean she had a nice smile and her laughter made you laugh with her, and she was so generous it was ridiculous, but she still wasn't the kind to make you fall," Tyler said.

Brock's restlessness grew. He stood, slowly agreeing again. "Right.''

"There was something about her, though," Tyler said, lowering his voice. "I bet she would be great in the sack. I wouldn't mind finding out my—''

The mere suggestion of his brother and Felicity made Brock's anger shoot through the roof. Around the table in two seconds, he wrapped his hands around Tyler's shirt. "If I ever catch you even touching her, even *thinking* about touching her—''

Tyler gave a gotcha grin. "Yep. I'd say you're about as attached to Felicity as the kids are. The last time you almost slugged me we were teenagers.''

Embarrassment mingled with anger. Brock sucked in a mind-clearing breath and swore. "You dog.''

"Woof-woof. Let go of my shirt so I can eat. If the woman is this deep under your skin, you might have to do something about it.''

"Ban her from the house," Brock said, shoving his hands in his pockets.

"Try explaining that to the kids if you want an insurrection on your hands.''

Brock sighed, remembering how effectively he'd pushed her away the night before she left. He'd denigrated their passion. The truth left a bitter taste in his mouth and yawning emptiness in his soul.

"I might not have to ban her," Brock said. "She really might not come back."

Later that night, Brock couldn't sleep. Again, he thought in disgust. He strolled down the hall to the guest room and pushed open the door. Her belongings were gone. It was almost as if she'd never been there. If not for the lingering hint of her scent and the images that assailed him, he could tell himself she hadn't made a true impact on him.

Sure she'd made him ache and want, but he knew better than to give his heart and soul to a woman like Felicity. He knew better than to give his heart to a woman, period. Even if he was tempted, there was a reason not to love a woman. The Logan Curse.

He remembered a time when he'd laughed at it, when he'd been arrogant and totally certain the curse wouldn't affect him. In fact, he'd been so full of himself he'd thought he held the power to break the curse.

That had been before his disastrous marriage, before he'd placed his trust in a woman and been proven so terribly wrong. That had been before his ex-wife had left him and the kids.

Brock felt a whisper of cool air whistle through him. He would never put himself and his children in such a vulnerable position again. It was best that she had left, he told himself, and best that she not return.

Felicity sipped the morning cappuccino her housekeeper, Anna, had brought her and looked out her penthouse bedroom window as she lounged in bed and stroked her white Persian cat Tia. The throngs of New Yorkers on the street looked like busy ants. Now that she'd given her deposition and conducted her business, everyone had somewhere to go except her.

Oh, she'd received oodles of invitations to lunch and charity events and parties, but the prospect of going to any of them didn't do a thing for her. In the overall scheme of things, she didn't feel like anyone in New York really needed her. If pressed, she would say the two who had missed her most in her absence were Anna and Tia.

"Pretty doggone pathetic," she muttered, choosing one of Bree's Texan terms.

She thought of Bree and Jacob and felt a strong tug. Strange how she'd only been at the Triple L three weeks, but she'd felt more a sense of belonging there than she ever had in her life.

Except with Brock.

Anger and hurt sliced through her. Restless, she walked over to the window. "Jerk, idiot," she said to herself. "Meany."

Felicity hadn't developed a tremendous amount of feminine pride along the way in her life, but the last few weeks she'd seen parts of herself she hadn't known existed, parts she liked. Her burgeoning pride told her if Brock didn't want her in his bed, then she wouldn't inflict herself on him.

Even if she missed him and wished he would look at her and fall half as desperately in love with her as she had with him.

She frowned, distantly hearing the phone ring. She would let Anna take the call. It was probably another invitation to a charity fashion show or dinner.

"Miss Chambeau," Anna said from her doorway. "Dr. Tyler Logan is on the line. He insists on speaking with you."

Felicity's heart squeezed. She immediately wondered if there'd been an emergency, if someone had been hurt. She picked up the phone. "Tyler?"

"Hey, Princess Felicity, what are you doing?"

Her lips twitched at his nickname for her. "Drinking cappuccino. And you?"

"I'm at the hospital."

She impatiently waited a few seconds. "And the purpose of your call?"

"I'm calling you with a message from a boy and girl in Texas."

Felicity's heart softened. "Bree and Jacob."

"Yep, they've got this wild idea that you're not coming back and they're pretty upset. I guess the best way to sum it up is to say you are missed."

"I'm not sure Brock would agree," she said.

"Brock's not an easy nut to crack. Persistence is the name of the game with him. You have to wear him down. I speak from personal experience."

Felicity heard the edge of humor in his voice, but felt no corresponding amusement. Brock had almost as much told her he didn't care whether she returned or not, and that still hurt.

"You're not talking," Tyler prompted.

"I'm thinking."

"Are you in love with my brother?" Tyler asked, cutting to the chase.

"Yes," Felicity answered because it was terrible, but it was the truth.

"And you want to marry him," Tyler continued. "So what you need to do is—"

"I never said I wanted to get married," Felicity interjected.

Silence stretched between them. Tyler chuckled. "You'll have to excuse me, but that's the first time I've ever heard a woman say she didn't want to get married. Where's the problem? He doesn't want to get married and neither do you. Sounds like a perfect match."

"The problem is he doesn't love me and even if a miracle happened, he would never admit it. You may not understand this, but it's not easy going where you're not wanted."

"Ah," Tyler said. "Your breeding is showing. In Texas, we believe that if what you want doesn't make you sweat, then it probably ain't worth a damn, anyway. But you probably don't know much about sweat, do you?"

Felicity felt a wave of indignation. She felt both insulted and challenged. "That was low. I believe Bree would call those fightin' words."

Tyler gave a dirty laugh. "When can we expect you back?"

"I'm thinking," she said, unwilling to give him the satisfaction. "Why are you pushing?"

"I don't play the role of brother's keeper very often because Brock is one of the most self-contained self-reliant men in the world. In this case, he's got a blind spot, so it's my duty to look after him."

Felicity's heart tightened. "And his blind spot is?"

"He needs you."

Eleven

Go get her, Tyler had told him last night. *You need her.* Brock shook his head as he paced the porch. He needed Felicity like he needed a rash. Since she'd left, he'd been distracted and hadn't slept well. It wasn't, however, because she had left, Brock told himself. It was because she had come into their lives in the first place. He had been just fine before she'd arrived.

His life had been peaceful.

Boring, his conscience chided.

No passions had kept him awake at night.

Sexually dead.

His emotions had remained on an even keel.

Emotionally in a coma.

Brock swore. He'd been listening to Tyler too much lately. He was too miserable to consider the possibility that Felicity had been good for him. He was disgusted with himself.

Resting his hands on his hips, he looked out on the horizon and reminded himself of his destiny. He had too many responsibilities, too many people depending on him to go chasing after a woman. If his responsibilities rode a little heavy on him and he chafed at the restrictions, he would get over it. He always did.

That should settle it. He wondered why it didn't. He wondered why he felt like a lonesome hound dog.

"Daddy?"

Brock turned to find his daughter in the doorway. She was twirling her hair with her finger, something she often did when she was upset. "What do you need, sweetheart?"

"Would you play 'Chopsticks' with me?"

His heart turned and he gave a half smile. "Sure. While we're at it, maybe I can show you a new tune, too."

He allowed her to lead him to the library. He sat down with her and played the baby grand with his daughter, and felt a bittersweet mix of memories. After a few minutes, Jacob poked his head in the room, and the three of them banged out "Chopsticks." It made him smile to think of how proud his mother would be to see that both his children had a measure of her musical talent.

He had started to show them the melody of "Heart and Soul" when he heard the click of high heels. He inhaled a wisp of perfume and his heartbeat picked up while his fingers slowed. He turned to find Felicity just inside the door. His heart slammed into his rib cage. She wore a cream-colored dress that faithfully followed her curves, but her facial expression was what gave him pause. If her eyes could talk they would have said, ''I dare you to love me.'' The kids squealed and yelled. ''Felicity! You're back!''

Brock noticed the white cat Felicity held with her right arm. What the hell was she doing bringing a cat here?

Bree and Jacob scrambled off the bench to see her. Bree threw her arms around Felicity's waist. ''I told Daddy you would come back. He said you might not. But I told him you would.''

''Can I hold your cat?'' Jacob asked. ''What's his name?''

''Tia is a she,'' she said with a smile and hug for both of them as she handed him the cat. ''And she's an indoor cat. She's didn't like the plane ride, so I'm sure she would love it if you sat down and held her.'' She knelt down and squeezed both kids' shoulders. ''I've missed you terribly.''

Jacob kicked at the floor. ''We, uh, missed you, too.''

Bree held up her fingers and wiggled them. ''My manicure is all gone.''

''I bombed my last book report,'' Jacob reluctantly admitted.

Brock felt a lump in his throat at his children's response to her. It was as if she brought the sunshine in the room with her. For them. For him?

She glanced up and walked toward him. She skimmed her hand over the top of the piano in a way that reminded him of the night he'd made love to her in this same room. ''I heard you playing. Sounded pretty good.''

Brock felt an odd kick of joy and pain. He had schooled himself to believe she wouldn't return. "What made you bring the cat?"

"Because I'm going to be here for a while. You told me you would help me find someone to set up my fund for me." She gave a heartbreaker's smile. "You weren't planning on reneging, were you?"

"No," he said, feeling his gut tighten just because she was here. His hands itched to take her in his arms. He stood and deliberately hooked his thumbs in his belt loops.

"Every time I decide you're heartless you do something to change my mind," she announced.

"Such as?"

"Such as play 'Chopsticks' with your kids." Her gaze went from sweet to womanly in an instant as she gave him a long once-over from head to toe. Brock felt it everywhere in between. She stretched up on her toes, almost close enough to kiss him, and Brock held his breath.

"It's good to see you," she whispered, then took a step back.

He ached to pull her against him and kiss her, to scold her for staying away so long, to fuss at her for standing too far away from him, but he bit his tongue. There was something different about her, he decided. It was as if she'd found something in New York; confidence or power or something like that. Whatever it was, it made him want her more badly than he ever had.

A little later, after Felicity had kissed the kids goodnight and he had tucked them in, Brock walked past her cracked-open doorway. He wasn't sure whether it was an invitation or not, but the temptation to look at her one more time tonight was irresistible.

He nudged the door and she glanced up with a guilty expression on her face. "Long day. Chocolate therapy. Want some?" she asked, nodding toward the piece of chocolate pie in her hand.

"That's okay," he said, stepping into her room thinking he wanted a helluva lot more from her than pie. He drank in the sight of her.

Her hair damp from a shower, she wore the silk robe he'd removed from her twice before. Her skin glowed in the soft light from the bedside lamp and her eyes held secrets he wanted to know.

"How was your trip?"

"Productive," she said, taking a small bite and closing her eyes as she savored it. "The deposition was boring, but necessary, and I kinda fired my financial advisors."

Brock raised his eyebrows. "You fired them?"

"I told them I was tired of arguing with them about funding my charitable trust, so they could either manage half of my money or they could manage none." She smiled and opened her eyes. "They did the math and chose half."

He leaned against the wall. "It was that easy?"

"Oh, no. They gave the regular manipulative line about how long they've worked for my family, close to a century, and how they knew much more about financial matters than I did and how I should respect my parents' wishes. It used to work like a charm."

"Why didn't it work this time?"

"I'm not sure. It was either sex or Texas."

Brock blinked. "What?"

"The reason it didn't work is either because I had sex with you or because being in Texas gave me a different perspective. I didn't feel incompetent and inferior anymore."

"What does that have to do with having sex with me?"

She looked away from him thoughtfully. "My passion was like a room inside me that I'd kept locked. Since you, I've found a part of myself that I didn't know was there, and it's incredibly powerful for me." She met his gaze. "I think that's why I was upset when you called what was between us *fun*. Are you sure you don't want a bite of pie?"

Brock felt a nagging sensation at his temples. "Lord help me, I think I've opened Pandora's box."

"What do you mean?"

"I mean if you think having sex gave you power, then you might also get the hare-brained notion that having sex with any man will give you power," Brock said, feeling his stomach turn at the prospect.

"You mean it won't?"

He suspected she was jerking his chain and it worked. "You're damn straight it won't. Sex with the wrong man will make you feel used and empty. Sex with the right man will make you feel special and powerful," he said, realizing that was how he felt when he made love with Felicity.

"Is it the same way with men?"

He shrugged. "I guess."

"So if it's the right person, he feels great, and if it's the wrong person, he doesn't. Where does fun fit in there?"

Uncomfortable with her questions and his own thoughts and feelings, Brock tapped his foot. Hell, he didn't know what to do with this woman and it didn't look like she was in a hurry to leave.

"You really look like you could use some chocolate therapy," she said, holding out a bite on the fork. "Here."

"Okay," he grumbled and sank down on the bed beside her. She fed him the bite and watched him swallow it.

"Is it so hard for you to say I'm more than fun for you? That you missed me just a little bit and you're glad to see me? Is it so hard?"

His throat tightened, making it difficult for him to swallow. "Yeah, it is."

"Because it's not true?"

Brock sighed and shook his head. "Because I don't want it to be true."

She reached for him, but he felt too raw and open. He rose from the bed and stood away from her. "You don't understand that it doesn't matter what I want. Maybe it's genetic. The Logans just don't fare well in the romance department. The end is the same. We all lose."

The next day, Felicity sat on the porch swing and read a book on charitable trusts. The material was so complicated she made notes as she went along because she was determined to become better informed. She had made it through the third chapter when a blue Mustang convertible pulled into the drive. A tall, slim dark-haired young woman got out of the driver's side and walked toward the porch.

It only took Felicity a moment to place the woman. She'd seen pictures of her on walls throughout the Logan house. A beautiful, feminine version of the Logans with long, wavy dark hair, lively blue eyes and a honey complexion. At the moment, her eyes looked tired and her complexion a little wan.

"Martina," she said. "Your brothers will be thrilled."

"The prodigal daughter returns home for a visit from Chicago," Martina said with a wry smile. "You must be Felicity. Tyler told me you've got Brock all stirred up. Just what he needs. On behalf of the rest of the Logans, thank you."

Felicity laughed. "I don't think he would agree with your philosophy."

"He'll come around," she said.

"You're prettier than your picture," Felicity said. "But I bet you're tired from your drive. Would you like something to drink?"

"Good idea," Martina said, pulling the door open. "And maybe some crackers."

Addie fussed over Martina and served the two women soda and crackers at Martina's request. "So when are you going to get a ring through Brock's nose and haul him to the altar?"

Felicity shook her head. "I haven't really been interested in getting married."

"Oh, that's right," Martina said. "You're loaded, so you don't need to tie yourself to a man, especially to a stubborn cuss like my brother."

"That's not exactly it, either. It's hard to explain."

"Try," Martina said, and Felicity heard Brock's bluntness in her tone.

"It's going to sound hokey to you, but I have this feeling of destiny about Brock. Like part of the reason I was put on this planet was to love him."

A dozen emotions shifted in Martina's eyes, but she nodded her head. "I can understand that," she said quietly.

"But Brock is convinced there's some kind of curse."

"Oh, yeah, he's a little fixated on that. You might have to get pushy with him."

"I may ask you more about that another time. You must forgive me for staring, but you look so much like the picture of your mother in the library."

Martina's eyes widened. "You've been inside the tomb? How'd you manage that?"

"I was forbidden to go near the men's quarters and I was told not to bother Addie and I can't drive."

Martina made a face. "Geez, he really put out the red carpet for you, didn't he?"

"I explored the house."

"I haven't been in that room in ages."

"I changed it a little."

Curiosity flickered in her eyes. "I want to see it. Let's go look."

Felicity led the way down the hall, pushed open the door and stepped aside for Martina to enter the room first.

"Oh, wow. There's light in here, and plants." She put her hand to her throat. "Sheet music on the piano. Do you play?"

"Some," Felicity conceded. "I've taught Bree and Jacob a few little songs."

Martina glanced up at the picture of the cocked gun

above the desk which Felicity had turned to face the wall. She snickered. "I like your attitude."

"Brock hasn't said anything yet."

"Good." She walked to the wall where her mother's picture hung and fell silent.

The grief and longing on Martina's face made Felicity feel as if she should turn away to give her privacy.

"I still wish I'd known her, maybe more now than I ever did," she said softly. "I used to sneak in here and sit and look at her picture and wonder how she would have talked to me, if she would have hugged me a lot or scolded me. One time my father caught me poking at the piano keys and he spanked me. I think I was an everyday reminder of his loss because I looked so much like her." She shook her head as if to shake off the thought and looked at the piano, then Felicity. "Will you play something?"

"Sure," Felicity said and sat down on the bench. "What would you like to hear?"

"You pick."

Felicity tried to think of something Brock's mother might have played. She chose Gershwin, a tune that combined sweetness and power. She let the music soar through her until the song ended. The silence was full of emotion. She glanced up at Martina and saw tears in her eyes. Her heart clutched. "I'm sorry. I didn't mean to upset you."

Martina swiped at her eyes and lifted her hand in protest. "It's not you. It's the room, the ranch, the memories. I must be a little more tired than I thought I was." She hesitated. "That song you played was beautiful. I always wanted to play because I knew my mother did, but my father wouldn't let anyone touch the piano after she died. This may sound strange, but I know she played the piano while she was pregnant with me. I've always wondered if I heard her play before I was born.''

She rolled her eyes and swiped at them again. ''Don't mind me. I've been driving too long. I think I'll go lie down.'' She glanced around the room, then back at Felicity. ''That destiny thing you were talking about may be true. You've brought the music back into this house.''

That evening, Brock, Tyler and the kids were beside themselves with excitement at Martina's arrival. While they talked, Felicity excused herself to the kitchen and planned a dinner party with Addie.

Brock walked up behind them. ''We'll be lucky if we can keep her here for two days,'' he told them.

''That's why we're planning it for tomorrow evening,'' Felicity said. ''We'll keep it simple—barbecue, baked potatoes, cole slaw and dessert served on paper plates. Addie says you have the tables. All we need is a decent sound system.''

''You sound like you've done this before,'' Brock said.

''My mother gave parties all the time. I learned by osmosis.'' She gave a cheeky smile. ''Another one of my highly marketable skills.''

He slid her an amused sideways glance, then after Addie left the room, he pulled her aside. ''Did Martina say anything about being sick?''

''No. She just said she was worn out from driving. Why?''

He frowned. "I don't know. Something doesn't seem right."

"Maybe after she gets a full night of rest, she'll seem better."

"Maybe," he agreed, still distracted.

"You know, Brock, seeing how much you care for your sister makes a big impression on me."

Surprise flickered through his eyes. "It does?"

She nodded. "I just wish I knew how to get you to care for me like that."

His eyes darkened with emotion and he touched a strand of her hair. "I care for you in other ways," he murmured. "Too much."

Longing for his touch for too long, she turned her cheek against his palm. He rubbed his thumb over her mouth and she parted her lips, tasting him with her tongue. When he slid his thumb just past her lips, she sucked it lightly.

Brock swore under his breath. He pulled his hand away and replaced it with his mouth, taking her lips with need so strong it bordered on desperation. Felicity couldn't help but respond. He was the man she was meant to love; she could feel it in every pore of her body. Every fiber of her being craved to be with him.

Brock lifted his mouth away to catch his breath, meshing his forehead with hers. He deliberately rocked himself against her. She could feel him hard and aroused against her. "What in hell are you trying to do to me?"

Felicity ran her fingertips up his arms all the way to his shoulders. It felt as if it had been forever since she'd held him. "The same thing you're doing to me," she finally managed.

He shook his head, skimming his lips across her forehead, wrapping his hand around the nape of her neck beneath her hair. "I can't get close enough to you."

"Then come closer," she told him.

He groaned. "You are frustrating the hell out of me."

Felicity shook her head, which was growing cloudy from his proximity. "You've got your pronouns mixed up," she said, pressing her open mouth to his neck. "I'm not frustrating you, Brock. *You* are frustrating you."

Twelve

The party went over like gangbusters. Everyone enjoyed the food and Martina caught up with some former school chums. It was a clear, warm night and the sound system worked like a dream.

Brock, however, was not in a festive mood. He still had an itchy feeling about Martina, Tyler had given him some unwelcome news and Jay Parker was dancing with Felicity for the fourth time. Jay was teaching her the two-step, but Brock suspected he'd like to teach Felicity a few other things. His temperature rose just thinking about it. Inclined to boot his neighbor into next week, Brock cut in.

He gave Jay a curt nod. "I'll teach her," he said.

Felicity stumbled and Brock tightened his grip. "It will take me twice as long to learn with you," she said, mis-stepping again.

"Other foot," he coached.

Felicity groaned. "I have a hard time thinking clearly when I'm this close to you."

His gut tightened. "Why is that?"

"Because you mess up my insides," she said, almost missing again.

He inhaled her scent and relished the way she felt in his arms, thinking he could have gotten distracted, too, if he hadn't been doing the two-step since he was a kid. "Just concentrate."

She took a breath and focused her gaze on his throat. "Okay, don't talk unless you have to. I'll pretend you're—"

Brock swore. "—don't say Tyler. If you mention his sorry name, I might throw you over my shoulder and—" Brock broke off and frowned.

Felicity smiled. "Go on," she said, the sexy dare glinting in her eyes again. "You were getting to the good part."

"Forget it," he muttered, but his contrary mind finished the scenario he started. Haul Felicity off to his bedroom and lose himself in her.

She stopped and looked up at him, lifting her hand to touch his cheek. "What's bothering you?"

Brock sighed. The way she asked the simple question was like a velvet arrow to his heart. He wondered how she had come to know him so well when he hadn't made it easy for her.

"Tyler just told me he's taking a position at a medical center in Fort Worth," Brock said. "He specialized in pediatric cardiology and he feels like he's spinning his wheels here. I can see his point, but I had to fight Dad like hell to let Tyler go to medical school.

The deal was he would return to practice near the Triple L."

"And he did," she said, "for a while."

"Yeah." He looked at Felicity and grew tired of struggling to keep his distance. "Something's not right with Martina. I can't put my finger on it, but I can tell something's not right."

"Why don't you ask her?"

"I did, but she denied it." Brock saw Jay Parker headed in their direction and swore under his breath. He tugged Felicity away from the crowd toward a stand of trees. "It sure as hell doesn't help my peace of mind that you're dancing with every man at the party."

"I was told by your daughter that you needed a woman to drive you a little crazy."

"You're doing a damn fine job," he said, and took her in his arms and kissed her. He pulled her close and submerged himself in the scent and sensation of her, her silky hair and responsive body. He took her mouth the same way he wanted the rest of her. He devoured her.

She wanted him. He could taste it in her mouth, feel it in every move of her body, hear it in her sighs. Her wanting fueled his, and the heat rose between them.

He pulled back slightly and swore again.

"You need to be careful or I might start thinking I'm special to you," she said breathlessly.

"Well, you are," Brock said, thoroughly displeased. "I'm not happy about it, and I'm not sure what to do with you."

"I have suggestions," she said, boldly lowering her hand to the straining fly of his jeans.

Brock was torn. He'd spent the last week in misery, denying himself permission to be close to her. When she'd returned from New York, it had taken every bit of his restraint not to ask her to move into his room.

"We don't have time," he said reluctantly, although he couldn't stop her caress.

She rubbed her lips across his, sending his arousal into third gear. "Time for what?"

"I have to check on some cattle tonight. It's a full moon and that always makes them drop." He caught her mouth with his and tasted her again.

Felicity eased his zipper down and Brock sucked in his breath. "What are you doing?" he whispered.

"Showing you how much I want you."

She wrapped her hand around him and Brock shuddered. "I want this to be a two-way street," he said. "We don't have time."

She rolled her hand over the honeyed tip of him and lifted her thumb to her tongue to taste his essence. It was so intimate and unbearably seductive. Brock couldn't have turned away from her if he had tried.

He took her mouth again, and she returned to his aching masculinity and began to pump and caress him. The tension in him built. He slid his hands under her dress, needing to touch her feminine secrets. He made love to her mouth with his and made her tremble with his hands, but it wasn't enough.

Her soft sounds of encouragement took him over the edge, and he spilled himself into her hand, holding her tight. He couldn't recall a woman demonstrating her love for him in such an intimate way. In some ways, what they'd just done felt more intimate than sex, and he felt oddly vulnerable. He tugged a handkerchief from his pocket, gave it to her and helped pull both of them back together. Then he pulled her into his arms and held her.

Felicity relaxed against him. "We need to go back, don't we?"

"Yeah," he said, not moving.

She glanced up at him, her heart in her eyes. "You know I'm in love with you."

Brock's heart squeezed so tight he could barely breathe. He'd dodged the truth of her feelings for him almost as successfully as he'd dodged his for her. Her feelings for him, however, showed in what she did and how she looked at him. The words shouldn't have been a surprise, but he still felt caught off guard. He knew he was holding something precious in his arms, but the shadow of the Logan Curse still haunted him.

After half a night spent out in the pasture, Brock rose late the next morning and stepped into the hall-way at the same time Tyler did.

His brother shot him a wary glance. "Well, are you speaking to me yet, or not?"

"I haven't decided. I need some coffee first. Are you headed down?"

Tyler nodded, and opened his mouth to speak, but the sound of someone in the hall bathroom made both turn in that direction. Brock winced. It sounded as if someone was sick.

"One of the kids?" he mused, then his mind clicked. "Martina. I knew something was wrong."

"But she said she was okay."

"And she'll lie to keep us from worrying about her," Brock said, truly worried now. He led the way down the hall to the bathroom. He heard running water. ''Martina Celia Logan,'' he called. ''Tyler and I are waiting for an explanation when you can haul your sick self out of there.''

The water stopped. ''Well, that makes me want to rush right out. Can't a girl puke in peace around here?''

''We can take down this door,'' Tyler said. ''No problem.''

''And you wonder why I don't come home often,'' she said, pulling the door open and glaring at both of them.

Brock's stomach twisted at her pale complexion. ''What's wrong?''

''Nothing terminal,'' she said.

Tyler frowned. ''Do better or I'll take you with me to the hospital.''

''I knew there was something wrong,'' Brock said.

Martina sighed. ''It's the scar,'' she said. ''Ever since you got your face torn up pulling me from that bull pen, you've always known when things were wrong with me.''

''You're stalling. Spill it,'' Brock said, growing more concerned with each passing moment.

She tried for a smile and failed. ''I'm pregnant.''

Brock felt his blood rush to his feet. *''Pregnant!''*

''How far along?'' Tyler asked. ''Have you seen a doctor?''

''Just two months. Yes, I've seen one, and I'll be looking for a new doctor as soon as I get to Dallas.''

''What happened to Chicago?''

''I got a transfer to Dallas.''

''I wondered why she drove,'' Tyler said.

"Why don't you live here?" Brock asked.

Martina rolled her eyes. "It would take me a year to list the reasons. Big one, however, is I want medical benefits throughout the pregnancy, which means I need to stay with my current company. I think that's enough questions for now, so—"

"Who's the father?"

In one second, Martina lost the color she'd gained by arguing with him and Tyler. Brock sensed whoever it was had hurt her badly. The pain etched on her face stabbed at him. In that moment, he remembered her as a scrappy little girl trying like the dickens to win her daddy's heart, and never quite succeeding.

"I have a logical explanation," she said in a serious voice.

"Which is," Tyler prompted.

"The stork did it."

Tyler rolled his eyes. "Now the real explanation," he said.

"Let's just say I made a mistake. I trusted when I shouldn't have."

"Who was it?" Brock demanded, wanting to find the guy and rip out his tonsils and other assorted organs.

Her face closed up tight. "Don't badger me about this. I'll tell you if and when I'm ready. I'm going back to bed." She gave a wry smile and turned away. "Have a nice day."

Feeling helpless, Brock watched her return to her room. If there was one emotion that he hated above all others and that made him irritable, it was feeling helpless. Biting back an oath, he stomped downstairs and ate breakfast. Tyler grabbed a cup of coffee and left while Brock stewed over Martina.

Felicity stepped into the room and smiled at him. "Good morning. New calves?"

Upset and frustrated, he refused to allow himself to feel soothed by her. He'd rather kick something. "Yeah, it was a full night."

She raised her eyebrows at his gruff tone and laid her hand on his shoulder. "Not enough sleep?"

He shrugged it off. "No," he said, standing. "Today will be busy, too. Tell Addie not to hold dinner for me."

Surprise and a sliver of hurt darkened her eyes. "Is something else wrong?"

He clamped his hat on his head. "Just my family going to hell in a handbasket. The Logan Curse has hit Martina. You can be sure I'm not riding that horse again," he told her, and tried to harden his heart when he saw the pain on her face. "Don't love me, Felicity. You'll just get hurt."

An hour later, Felicity had hugged the kids as they left for school, stared at the same page of a book for twenty minutes, and she was still reeling from Brock's words. She had thought he'd taken a step toward her last night. Had she been so wrong? Had her instincts been that far off?

She glanced up to see Martina walking down the steps with her luggage. Surprise rippled through her. "You're leaving so soon?"

Martina nodded. "After my announcement this morning, I need to give Brock and Tyler some time to adjust. Toast,'' she said, moving toward the kitchen. "Toast and tea."

Confused, Felicity followed her. "Your announcement?"

"You haven't heard," Martina said, putting bread in the toaster and grabbing the kettle of hot water from the stove. "I'm sure you will. I'm pregnant and have no intention of revealing who the father is, let alone marrying him."

Stunned, Felicity simply stared. "Oh." She saw the ragged defiance on Martina's face and felt a connection with her. Felicity was defying her own odds by loving Brock. "You must have your reasons."

Martina relaxed slightly. "Thank you. I do." She put a tea bag in a mug, poured the hot water over it, then snatched the toast. "Before I leave, there was something I wanted to do with you."

"Learn a little song on the piano?"

Martina smiled. "No, although I'd like a rain check for that." She took a bite of toast and swallowed it. "I want you to drive me into town and bring your checkbook, birth certificate and another ID. In Texas, it's always good when a woman has her own set of wheels. It keeps a man on his toes, and my brother has had it too easy too long with you."

Felicity felt a rush of excitement. "You're taking me to get a license."

"Actually you're gonna drive, so we'll both be sure you can get back. It's the least I can do for someone who has worked miracles in this household."

Four hours later, Felicity and Martina sat in a diner on the corner of Main Street and, with a soda, toasted Felicity's driver's license and the purchase of her first car, a white Bronco. "It was worth the line at the Department of Public Safety to see the look on that salesman's face when you said you were buying with cash and if he didn't want to sell you a car, you would find someone who would." She chuckled. "Now, you will truly be able to drive Brock crazy."

Felicity's euphoria dissipated. "I wish you weren't leaving."

Martina sobered. "I never had a sister, but if I could have wished for one, I think I would have wished for you. Who knows? Maybe I'll be able to call you sister someday," she said with a half smile that reminded Felicity of Brock. "In the meantime, I need to go, but I will be back."

"Brock will worry about you. So will I."

"Brock always worries about me. He thinks it's his job. Maybe you can distract him."

"Sometimes I'm not sure. It's like he's got this wall around him, and I try to tap at it and I make a little progress, but then he rebuilds it."

"Sometimes tapping doesn't work. Sometimes you just have to burn the barrier down to the ground, and if there's anyone who can do that for Brock, it's you."

Despite a busy day, Brock made it home for dinner that night, but Felicity was nowhere in sight. He wondered if he should apologize for his runaway mouth, but he still felt the weight of the damn Logan Curse hanging around his neck. His resentment against his heritage burned like a branding iron. Now Martina was affected by it, too. The brat had skipped town this morning, but at least she'd shown enough consideration to call and tell him she'd arrived safely in Dallas.

He didn't see Felicity that night or the following morning, but he carried her image with him throughout the day. He wondered if he always would. After a Cattle Ranchers' Association meeting, he arrived home and scouted the downstairs living areas for her. Fighting a hollow disappointment when he didn't find her, he decided to take a long shower and go to bed early.

After his shower, he dried off and looped a towel around his waist. He opened the bathroom door into his bedroom and stopped at the sight of lit candles all over his room. He inhaled the scents of vanilla, cinnamon, and Felicity. His gaze shot to his bed and he saw her sitting with her legs crossed, her expression expectant. His heartbeat picked up. He was so relieved to see her a shudder rippled through him.

"What's this?" he asked, waving his hand at the candles.

"It's a special occasion," she said, her eyes mysterious. There was a determined, provocative air about her that plucked at something deep inside him. She stood and moved toward him. "Are you glad to see me?"

Her gaze dared him to tell the deep, dark truth. Tired of denying himself, he took a deep breath. "Yes."

"Tell me something," she said, lifting her hand to his shoulder. "Have you ever felt lonely for me?"

Brock's stomach tightened. He thought of last night and the day before when he'd spent the entire day longing for her. He thought of the empty days and nights when she'd been in New York. He thought of all the days before he'd even met her that he had longed for someone like Felicity, and his mouth went dry at the ominous realization of how important she was to him.

"Yes," he finally said. "I think I've been lonely for you most of my life."

Her eyes widened and turned shiny with unshed tears. "Don't be lonely for me again, Brock. You never ever need to be."

He pulled her against him and inhaled her scent. He wanted to inhale everything about her so he could feel her all the time. He nuzzled her hair and glanced at the flicker of the dozens of candles. "What is the special occasion?"

She pulled back slightly and looked at him with a love so fierce it burned. "We're going to break a curse tonight," she said and sealed her intention with a kiss that rocked him to his soul.

She made love to him like a firestorm, burning away his doubt and lighting every dark corner inside him. With her hands, tongue and body, she made him want until he could barely stand it. A seductive tease, she tenderly, yet mercilessly drove him mad.

Their bodies slick with sweat, hearts pounding against each other, breaths coming in fits and starts, he turned the tables and teased her the way she had him, toying with her sensitive body, taking her to the edge with his tongue. It wasn't enough to take her to the top once. He took her again and again until she pleaded with him to come inside her. Brock did and with the joining, he could almost swear he heard mountains crumble. Afterward, he wrapped her in his arms, and they slept that way through the night.

When Brock awakened the next morning, Felicity

was still in his arms, her legs entwined with his, her breath flowing in a soft rhythm against his neck. He couldn't remember when he'd awakened with a heart so full of hope.

Pulling back slightly, he looked at the way the sunlight shining through his curtain danced over her. He kissed her head. Maybe, just maybe, the curse was truly broken.

Thirteen

Felicity awakened to the sight of a bluebonnet next to her cheek on Brock's pillow. Her heart took a dip. She sat up in bed and her body immediately reminded her of their powerful lovemaking the night before.

Brock loved her.

Her life had never been more right. She picked up the bluebonnet and smiled.

After a light breakfast, she showered, dressed, and studied her book on charitable trusts. Brock might think she was silly, but Felicity wanted to see him, to make sure she hadn't dreamed last night.

Fixing a picnic lunch, she asked for the calmest horse in the stable and with directions from a ranch hand, she set out to surprise Brock. It was a glorious day, warm and bright with sunshine. Sally, the mare, was gentle, and Felicity was bubbling over with the prospect of seeing Brock again. Humming, she didn't see the rattlesnake until they were almost on it.

Her heart lurching into her throat, she tried to guide the horse away, but the rattler jerked. The horse reared high and Felicity clung to the reins. The mare reared again, neighing, then bucking. Felicity lost her grip, and went airborne.

She cried out, desperately reaching, then hit the ground. Everything went black.

Brock stood in the hospital emergency waiting room unable to shake the image of Felicity lying in the grass so utterly still. The ride to the hospital had been interminable.

This couldn't be happening, he thought. The threat of the Logan Curse taunted, but he brushed it aside. Felicity wouldn't want him thinking about some damn curse right now.

Tyler approached him with a concerned expression on his face. "You can see her, but she's still not conscious. No broken bones, but she took a hard knock on the head."

"Will she be okay?"

"The longer she takes to wake up, the more we have to think about complications," Tyler said, leading Brock to the examination room.

Brock had thought his stomach couldn't sink lower than when he'd seen her on the ground. "What complications?"

"Hemorrhage, coma," Tyler said in a low voice. "It's too early for that, though. You've gotta think positive."

He walked through the doorway and felt his heart

stop again at the sight of her. She looked as if she could wake up any minute and smile at him. Brock willed her to do just that, but she continued to lie perfectly still.

"Have a seat," Tyler said, scooting a chair closer to the bed. "You want some coffee?"

Brock sank into the chair, his gaze still fastened on her. "No."

He felt Tyler squeeze his arm before he left the room, and Brock rubbed his face, sick with regret. What a fool he'd been, wasting precious moments when he could have been happy, when Felicity could have been happy. He'd been too guarded to let her in.

"Wake up, Felicity," he said, taking her hand in his.

He'd been half-alive before Felicity had burst into his life. She'd shown him everything good about himself and made him want to be better than he was. She had loved him even when he rejected her.

His eyes burned with remorse and he did something he hadn't done in years. He prayed.

"God, let her live so I can tell her I'm sorry. So I can tell her I love her a dozen times a day for the rest of my life." He closed his eyes and felt a tear stream down his cheek. "So I can show her how special she is."

The darkness of the curse taunted him again, but again, Brock fought it off. He was not going to let her go.

"Wake up, Felicity," he said, his voice husky to his ears. "Wake up, and let me love you for the rest of my life."

He stared at her face, and her eyes fluttered open.

He blinked to make sure he hadn't imagined it. Her gaze was cloudy, but her eyes were open.

His heart leapt into his throat and he jumped from the chair to stand beside her. "Felicity!"

Disoriented, she furrowed her eyebrows. "Brock?"

He squeezed her hand. "I'm here. I'm right here, and I'm not leaving."

"What—" She shook her head and groaned.

"Stay still," he said, gently touching her head, feeling his eyes well up again. "You hurt your head."

"The snake," she murmured. "Did the snake get the horse?"

Brock worried she was suffering from delusions. "What snake?"

"The snake that scared the horse."

Realization trickled through his panicked mind. "No. Sally's fine. You got the raw end of the deal."

She closed her eyes and smiled wanly. "I wanted to surprise you with lunch. I loved the bluebonnet. It made me think of your eyes."

His chest tightened when she stopped talking. "Don't go to sleep," he said.

With obvious effort, she dragged her heavy lids open. "Why?"

"You scared the hell out of me. I was afraid of losing you."

"Silly," she said, closing her eyes again. "You're stuck with me."

Brock breathed a little then, but he didn't budge from her side the rest of the day, waking her frequently per the doctor's orders, even when she got cranky.

"My head feels like elephants are stomping through it. Why can't you let me rest?" she asked.

"Because the doctor wants to make sure you have all your faculties," Brock quoted.

"I forgot how irritating doctors can be. Can't you take me home?"

"Soon," he promised.

She sighed. "I want you to take me home, rid me of half of my money and—" She broke off, biting her lip.

"And what?"

"Never ever stop loving me."

Within twenty-four hours, Brock took care of her first two requests. After he brought her home, he arranged for a reputable attorney to make a house call. Although Felicity was much poorer by the time the man left, she grinned from ear to ear.

"Thank you, Brock. I can't tell you how important this is to me. Now my inheritance will do some good and I can get off the rich-lady list. Thank you."

"You're welcome," he said distractedly. He had one more matter to handle, and the thought of it made him sweat. The thought of not doing it, however, was untenable. "The other night you and I started the process of breaking the curse. I want us to finish it."

She pushed herself up among the pillows in his bed and met his gaze. "How?"

He took a deep breath and sat next to her on the bed. "I want you to marry me."

Surprise, joy and confusion widened her eyes. The confusion made his gut knot.

"You don't have to marry me for me to love you and stay with you."

"I know, but I want to be connected to you in every

possible way. I want you to belong to me, and I want to belong to you.''

''Are you sure you want me to be your official crazy-making woman?''

''As sure as my name is Logan.''

''I never felt like I belonged to anyone or anything until you. Yes, I'll marry you.''

His joy complete, Brock pulled her to him. This Manhattan troublemaker had taken him by storm, brought music back into his home, and broken the Logan Curse, at least for him. Thank God, he thought and knew he was holding a piece of heaven in his arms.

*   *   *   *   *

Watch for Tyler Logan's story in
THE DOCTOR WORE SPURS
the second book in Leanne Banks's
exciting miniseries

LONE STAR FAMILIES: THE LOGANS.

On sale in March from Silhouette Desire.
And now for a sneak preview of
THE DOCTOR WORE SPURS,
please turn the page.

The man with the cowboy hat waited patiently behind Jill Hershey's former client, Mr. Waldron. Jill tried not to look at him, but it was difficult. He was taller than most men in the room, unabashedly Western, and, she concluded after a few moments passed, determined. He was a little too handsome for his own good, she thought. Just the way he stood, he exuded a gut-level kind of confidence most people never experienced. His searching gaze generated an odd ripple inside her.

Her former client must have felt the man's presence because he glanced around quizzically.

The man immediately stepped forward. "Hello, I'm Dr. Tyler Logan from Fort Worth General Hospital. Pleased to meet you."

"Bill Waldron of Cincinnati University Hospital. This is—"

"Jill Hershey, public relations sorceress," Dr. Logan finished with enigmatic charm. He extended his hand and met her gaze with the direct impact of a two-by-four. "We need you."

Jill blinked. Although her career success had grown quickly over the last three years, she wasn't accustomed to this approach. Noticing the strength and size of his hand, she managed a smile. "I'm flattered," she said. "I think."

Mr. Waldron excused himself and Jill retrieved her hand. "I wouldn't call myself a sorceress."

"You don't have to. You have others who do it for you."

She felt a surge of curiosity. She wondered what was behind his cowboy charm. "Dr. Logan," she began.

"Call me Tyler," he said.

Surprise seeped through her. Many of the doctors she'd met were very attached to their titles. "Tyler, what is your specialty?"

"Pediatric cardiologist. Surgery."

Jill's stomach clenched. It took a moment to catch her breath, but with effort she produced a smile. "That's an important field, but I must tell you I haven't done much work with children's projects."

"Why not?"

His question took her off guard. "I always felt I was more effective with other specialties."

"You don't like kids?"

"No!" she immediately denied, and shook her head. "I—I—do like children." She shrugged, wanting to get away from this impertinent man who had unknowingly stabbed her in her most vulnerable area.

"I told you I have always felt I was more effective with other specialties. Not only that," she said, wishing her voice didn't sound so tight with tension, "my latest projects have been with larger hospitals."

"You wouldn't want to get in a rut," Tyler said.

Jill's head began to pound. "A rut?" she repeated.

He nodded. "You look like a woman who needs a new challenge to keep you happy."

She didn't know what irritated her more, the fact that he was making a huge assumption or the fact that it was right. "Dr. Logan—"

"Tyler," he corrected, his blue eyes glinting with masculine humor.

She stifled a sigh. "Tyler, I have to be honest. I usually accept assignments recommended by the president of my company. If you're interested in our services, you can contact him. Our telephone and fax numbers are in the conference kit. It was nice meeting you."

He nodded slowly, thoughtfully, as if he saw more than she wanted him to see. Jill turned away, both disturbed and relieved.

"I dare you," she heard from behind her. His words brought her back around.

"Pardon?"

"I dare you to come to Fort Worth General and make a lot of children's lives longer and better. You've got what it takes to do it." He looked her directly in the eye, and she felt the heat and power of his passion.

"I dare you."

Desire®

January 2000
HER FOREVER MAN
#1267 by Leanne Banks
Lone Star Families: The Logans

February 2000
A BRIDE FOR JACKSON POWERS
#1273 by Dixie Browning
The Passionate Powers

March 2000
A COWBOY'S SECRET
#1279 by Anne McAllister
Code of the West

April 2000
LAST DANCE
#1285 by Cait London
Freedom Valley

May 2000
DR. IRRESISTIBLE
#1291 by Elizabeth Bevarly
From Here to Maternity

June 2000
TOUGH TO TAME
#1297 by Jackie Merritt

MAN OF THE MONTH

For twenty years Silhouette has been giving you the ultimate in romantic reads. Come join the celebration as some of your favorite authors help celebrate our anniversary with the most sensual, emotional love stories ever!

Available at your favorite retail outlet.

Silhouette®
Where love comes alive™

Visit us at www.romance.net

SDMOM00

If you enjoyed what you just read,
then we've got an offer you can't resist!

Take 2 bestselling love stories FREE!

Plus get a FREE surprise gift!

Clip this page and mail it to Silhouette Reader Service™

IN U.S.A.
3010 Walden Ave.
P.O. Box 1867
Buffalo, N.Y. 14240 1867

IN CANADA
P.O. Box 609
Fort Erie, Ontario
L2A 5X3

YES! Please send me 2 free Silhouette Desire® novels and my free surprise gift. Then send me 6 brand-new novels every month, which I will receive months before they're available in stores. In the U.S.A., bill me at the bargain price of $3.12 plus 25¢ delivery per book and applicable sales tax, if any*. In Canada, bill me at the bargain price of $3.49 plus 25¢ delivery per book and applicable taxes**. That's the complete price and a savings of over 10% off the cover prices—what a great deal! I understand that accepting the 2 free books and gift places me under no obligation ever to buy any books. I can always return a shipment and cancel at any time. Even if I never buy another book from Silhouette, the 2 free books and gift are mine to keep forever. So why not take us up on our invitation. You'll be glad you did!

225 SEN CNFA
326 SEN CNFC

Name _____ (PLEASE PRINT)

Address _____ Apt.# _____

City _____ State/Prov. _____ Zip/Postal Code _____

* Terms and prices subject to change without notice. Sales tax applicable in N.Y.
** Canadian residents will be charged applicable provincial taxes and GST.
   All orders subject to approval. Offer limited to one per household.
® are registered trademarks of Harlequin Enterprises Limited.

DES99

©1998 Harlequin Enterprises Limited

Silhouette® *Desire*®

is proud to present a brand-new miniseries
by bestselling author

LEANNE BANKS

THE LOGANS
LONE STAR
FAMILIES

**Meet the Logans—
each a sexy blend of
power, brains and
strength. But what
each Logan seeks
most is that one great
love that lasts a
lifetime....**

On sale January 2000—**HER FOREVER MAN**
On sale March 2000—**THE DOCTOR WORE SPURS**
On sale May 2000—**EXPECTING HIS CHILD**

Look for all three of these irresistible stories of
love, heading your way in 2000—only from

Silhouette®
Where love comes alive™

Available at your favorite retail outlet.

Visit us at www.romance.net   SDLL

SILHOUETTE'S 20TH ANNIVERSARY CONTEST
OFFICIAL RULES
NO PURCHASE NECESSARY TO ENTER

1. To enter, follow directions published in the offer to which you are responding. Contest begins 1/1/00 and ends on 8/24/00 (the "Promotion Period"). Method of entry may vary. Mailed entries must be postmarked by 8/24/00, and received by 8/31/00.

2. During the Promotion Period, the Contest may be presented via the Internet. Entry via the Internet may be restricted to residents of certain geographic areas that are disclosed on the Web site. To enter via the Internet, if you are a resident of a geographic area in which Internet entry is permissible, follow the directions displayed on-line, including typing your essay of 100 words or fewer telling us "Where In The World Your Love Will Come Alive." On-line entries must be received by 11:59 p.m. Eastern Standard time on 8/24/00. Limit one e-mail entry per person, household and e-mail address per day, per presentation. If you are a resident of a geographic area in which entry via the Internet is permissible, you may, in lieu of submitting an entry on-line, enter by mail, by hand-printing your name, address, telephone number and contest number/name on an 8"x 11" plain piece of paper and telling us in 100 words or fewer "Where In The World Your Love Will Come Alive," and mailing via first-class mail to: Silhouette 20th Anniversary Contest, (in the U.S.) P.O. Box 9069, Buffalo, NY 14269-9069; (In Canada) P.O. Box 637, Fort Erie, Ontario, Canada L2A 5X3. Limit one 8"x 11" mailed entry per person, household and e-mail address per day. On-line and/or 8"x 11" mailed entries received from persons residing in geographic areas in which Internet entry is not permissible will be disqualified. No liability is assumed for lost, late, incomplete, inaccurate, nondelivered or misdirected mail, or misdirected e-mail, for technical, hardware or software failures of any kind, lost or unavailable network connection, or failed, incomplete, garbled or delayed computer transmission or any human error which may occur in the receipt or processing of the entries in the contest.

3. Essays will be judged by a panel of members of the Silhouette editorial and marketing staff based on the following criteria:

> Sincerity (believability, credibility)—50%
> Originality (freshness, creativity)—30%
> Aptness (appropriateness to contest ideas)—20%

Purchase or acceptance of a product offer does not improve your chances of winning. In the event of a tie, duplicate prizes will be awarded.

4. All entries become the property of Harlequin Enterprises Ltd., and will not be returned. Winner will be determined no later than 10/31/00 and will be notified by mail. Grand Prize winner will be required to sign and return Affidavit of Eligibility within 15 days of receipt of notification. Noncompliance within the time period may result in disqualification and an alternative winner may be selected. All municipal, provincial, federal, state and local laws and regulations apply. Contest open only to residents of the U.S. and Canada who are 18 years of age or older, and is void wherever prohibited by law. Internet entry is restricted solely to residents of those geographical areas in which Internet entry is permissible. Employees of Torstar Corp., their affiliates, agents and members of their immediate families are not eligible. Taxes on the prizes are the sole responsibility of winners. Entry and acceptance of any prize offered constitutes permission to use winner's name, photograph or other likeness for the purposes of advertising, trade and promotion on behalf of Torstar Corp. without further compensation to the winner, unless prohibited by law. Torstar Corp and D.L. Blair, Inc., their parents, affiliates and subsidiaries, are not responsible for errors in printing or electronic presentation of contest or entries. In the event of printing or other errors which may result in unintended prize values or duplication of prizes, all affected contest materials or entries shall be null and void. If for any reason the Internet portion of the contest is not capable of running as planned, including infection by computer virus, bugs, tampering, unauthorized intervention, fraud, technical failures, or any other causes beyond the control of Torstar Corp. which corrupt or affect the administration, secrecy, fairness, integrity or proper conduct of the contest, Torstar Corp. reserves the right, at its sole discretion, to disqualify any individual who tampers with the entry process and to cancel, terminate, modify or suspend the contest or the Internet portion thereof. In the event of a dispute regarding an on-line entry, the entry will be deemed submitted by the authorized holder of the e-mail account submitted at the time of entry. Authorized account holder is defined as the natural person who is assigned to an e-mail address by an Internet access provider, on-line service provider or other organization that is responsible for arranging e-mail address for the domain associated with the submitted e-mail address.

5. Prizes: Grand Prize—a $10,000 vacation to anywhere in the world. Travelers (at least one must be 18 years of age or older) or parent or guardian if one traveler is a minor, must sign and return a Release of Liability prior to departure. Travel must be completed by December 31, 2001, and is subject to space and accommodations availability. Two hundred (200) Second Prizes—a two-book limited edition autographed collector set from one of the Silhouette Anniversary authors: Nora Roberts, Diana Palmer, Linda Howard or Annette Broadrick (value $10.00 each set). All prizes are valued in U.S. dollars.

6. For a list of winners (available after 10/31/00), send a self-addressed, stamped envelope to: Harlequin Silhouette 20th Anniversary Winners, P.O. Box 4200, Blair, NE 68009-4200.

Contest sponsored by Torstar Corp., P.O. Box 9042, Buffalo, NY 14269-9042.

ENTER FOR
A CHANCE TO WIN*

Silhouette's 20th Anniversary Contest

Tell Us Where in the World
You Would Like *Your* Love To Come Alive...
And We'll Send the Lucky Winner There!

Silhouette wants to take you wherever
your happy ending can come true.

Here's how to enter: Tell us, in 100 words or less,
where you want to go to make your love come alive!

In addition to the grand prize, there will be 200
runner-up prizes, collector's-edition book sets
autographed by one of the Silhouette anniversary
authors: **Nora Roberts, Diana Palmer,
Linda Howard** or **Annette Broadrick**.

DON'T MISS YOUR CHANCE TO WIN!
ENTER NOW! No Purchase Necessary

Where love comes alive™

Name:

Address:

City: State/Province:

Zip/Postal Code:

Mail to Harlequin Books: **In the U.S.:** P.O. Box 9069, Buffalo, NY
14269-9069; **In Canada:** P.O. Box 637, Fort Erie, Ontario, L4A 5X3

*No purchase necessary—for contest details send a self-addressed stamped envelope to:
Silhouette's 20th Anniversary Contest, P.O. Box 9069, Buffalo, NY, 14269-9069 (include
contest name on self-addressed envelope). Residents of Washington and Vermont may
omit postage. Open to Cdn. (excluding Quebec) and U.S. residents who are 18 or over.
Void where prohibited. Contest ends August 31, 2000.

PS20CON_R